Fatal Little Lies

Loren Zahn

GREY CASTLE PUBLISHING

This book was published in the United States of America.

Fatal Little Lies is a work of fiction. Names, characters, institutions of higher learning, businesses, places, events and incidents are either the products of the author's imagination or used in a fictitious manner. Any resemblance to actual persons, living or dead, or actual events is purely coincidental.

Grey Castle Publishing
San Diego, California
http://www.Greycastlepublishing.com

ISBN-13: 978-0692958353
ISBN-10: 0692958355

Fatal Little Lies

GREY CASTLE PUBLISHING

Prologue

Theo Hunter held the phone long after the caller had clicked off.

Frank was missing. His FBI handler didn't sugarcoat the message. Theo wouldn't have wanted her to. Alex Thorkensen delivered it unadulterated and naked, to the point. "We haven't heard from Frank in a few weeks."

Theo knew that a "few weeks" in FBI lingo was the equivalent of "a too many months" in layman talk. Theo also knew that Frank was undercover, working a line on a human-trafficking operation on the Mexican border. Thorkensen said he'd missed several check-ins. Not a good sign.

"I thought you'd want to know." Alex said. "As soon as we know something, I'll be in touch."

"Thanks, Alex."

"Frank is smart and he's sharp, Theo. Sometimes . . ." Alex said, clearing her throat.

"Got it."

"Look, Theo, try not to worry."

"Worry is my middle name."

A Few Months Later

Theo slipped the ring off her finger and pressed it into the velvet slot in its box—the one Frank had pulled from his pocket the day he'd given it to her.

It was that day at the airport when he'd said that he couldn't imagine living his life anyone else, that they were right for each other because they wouldn't be right for anybody else.

Romantic without being gushy. Just like Frank.

The engagement ring's big diamond still sparkled with the promise of a life she and Frank had planned together. That was over now. Vanished. Just like Frank.

She snapped the lid shut, slid the box in the corner under some lingerie and shoved the drawer closed.

The act felt as absolute as closing the lid on a coffin. The ache it produced was raw and just as final.

1

San Diego

"You can do this, Theo," Sam Morley said. "These kids want to hear about the exciting and glamorous parts of investigative journalism. They can learn about the pressure cooker in the newsroom when, and if, they ever land a job. Right now, the industry needs a shot in the arm, an infusion of fresh blood! You can give it to 'em. Fire these kids up."

"I don't talk to journalism classes, Sam. I don't want to. I don't feel the urge to recruit new blood or any blood for that matter. You go. Just don't growl at them."

"Theo, this isn't a suggestion. It's an order!"

Theo had been at *The Tattler* ever since she was fired from San Diego's main newspaper, *The Chronicle*, for exposing a devious political takeover that made her a casualty of vicious politics. The aftermath was brutal. Sam Morley, *The Tattler's* editor-in-chief and no stranger to dirty political conspiracies, wasn't fooled. He brought her into the fold, gave her a job, and helped her restore her standing as a top-notch investigative journalist. In the process, Theo solved a series of vicious murders, stopped a maniacal killer targeting San Diego's pillars of society, and nearly lost her own life in the process. When Theo's in-depth reports made world and national headlines, *The Chronicle* begged her to return. She thumbed her nose at them and chose to stay with Morley and *The Tattler*. She'd been there ever since. That was going on nine years now.

To most, Morley wasn't your typical gruff editor with the heart of gold. He was just gruff. Building *The Tattler* into San Diego's popular weekly took savvy and guts. Morley had them both. Under his guidance, *The Tattler* snatched up an impressive market share of print media interest, especially among young professionals. Even the millennials, who typically shunned print media for crawlers' scrolling text at the bottom of a TV screen and Twitter news blasts, had become *Tattler* regulars. That was Sam's doing. He was proud of it and his staff. As Morley tells it, he grabbed Theo after her *Chronicle* debacle because she had a reporter's sharp analytical skills, and she was nosey—excellent qualities for an investigative snoop. Sam and Theo were a great team because they worked together like family—arguing, hanging up on each other's phone calls. Watching each other's backs.

"I'm surprised that San Diego State still offers journalism as a course of study. Where did they find students who want to work that hard?"

"Now, Theo, don't undersell them. Even Pulitzer Prize journalists were once snot-nosed rug rats."

"Why?"

"Why what?" Sam intoned in his best Jungian. "Why should you care? Or why should you go?"

"Are you trolling for new interns, Sam? Didn't the last batch run screaming from the newsroom, forever traumatized by your bellowing encouragement in four-letter profanities?"

"Now, Theo. You know I'm a pussycat."

"Bullshit!"

"Okay, enough of the pep talk. So. Class is at 7:30, in the 400 building, third floor, Room 312. *Introduction to Journalism.*"

"A.M.?"

"Yeah. Thanks, kiddo," Sam said and hung up.

"Wait! Sam! What the—? I didn't say I'd do it!" Theo yelled to the long-gone Sam.

The loaded elevator groaned its way to the third floor. Theo, her rolling cart chock-full of the latest *Tattler* edition, found Room 312. It was packed. The instructor was writing her name and title on the whiteboard.

"Excuse me," Theo said. "Mr. Fields?"

"I'm Tom Dawes," the whiteboard scribe said, turning to face her. "Mr. Fields is out this semester. Guess they didn't tell you that."

He dropped the black marker in the tray and extended his hand.

"Actually, Sam, my editor, didn't tell me. I picked up the name from the catalogue."

"Of course. No problem. Listen, thanks for coming. I've got to fill in down the hall. I'll be back in forty-five minutes. They've got lots of questions. So, I'll leave you to it."

With that, Dawes grabbed a notebook and a stack of papers and started for the door.

"Uh …," Theo stammered. "Where do you want me to start? What topics do you want me cover?"

Dawes looked back. "Tell them about your job. That should keep their attention."

With that, he was gone.

Theo stared at the packed classroom. All heads were turned in her direction, dozens of faces staring right back at her. She couldn't tell if they were enthusiastic or skeptical. She walked around to the front of the desk, leaned back and folded her arms.

"So, who wants to hear about … the murders?"

A sea of hands shot up.

2

Theo wondered where the time went when the bell rang signaling the end of the class. It had gone pretty well. The students asked pertinent and intelligent questions about her researching methods. A couple offered suggestions, which she thanked them for. Some asked for business cards on their way out. Most grabbed the free copies of *The Tattler*.

Theo didn't kid herself that it was the news content they wanted. *The Tattler* ran a high volume of advertisements—and coupons. She figured things hadn't changed much since her college days when she and most of her fellow students were rabid coupon-cutters looking for fast-food restaurant discounts. She was headed out the door when Tom Dawes showed up.

"Looks like you did okay," Dawes said.

"Yeah. It wasn't half-bad."

"Do you think you could come back another time?"

"No promises, Tom. I have to see what my schedule looks like. It all depends on the assignments Sam digs up. Figuratively."

He nodded understanding. "Well, thanks, again."

Theo smiled and headed down the corridor with her rolling cart many *Tattler* issues lighter. After a quick stop at the restroom, she caught the elevator. It wasn't crammed this time. There were only three other passengers, a student in a wheelchair, his attendant, and a middle-aged man who sported a full beard, and serious clothes. She pegged him for a professor. Theo nodded to her companions and they continued their descent to the lobby in typical elevator-etiquette silence.

On the ride down, Theo sensed that someone was sizing her up and hoped she wasn't trailing a sheet of toilet paper. As the doors opened to the lobby, she waited for the student in the wheelchair and his companion to head out before she exited. The bearded man waited. Making her way across the tiled lobby toward the double glass doors, Theo caught her reflection and, behind her, the elevator. Its door was still open, held by the bearded man watching her.

"Hey, Teach!" Abby yelled from her car as Theo pulled up in front of the *Las Casitas* complex.

"You got the Beemer running, I see," Theo barked over the vroom-vroom of the classic BMW 520i.

Abby switched off the engine as Theo walked up on the driver side. "Yeah. Helmut finally figured it out. Apparently, she was fitted with a Stromberg 175 CDET carburetor, the model sold in the UK. That was a big *no bueno* for my baby." Abby said, patting the steering wheel. "So, him being the German engineering genius he is, he refitted her with a dual Bosch L-jetronic fuel injection carburetor—a much better fit for her six-cylinder engine. Now, she purrs like a tigress in heat!"

Theo's lopsided smile didn't go unnoticed.

"What?" Abby said.

"Nothing. Nothing. Just you and cars. I swear, Abs, you should have been a mechanic."

Abby looked lovingly at her baby. "Yeah. I think I'd be good at it."

"How about some coffee?" Theo said. "I could do with a little unwind."

"No time, kiddo. I'm already late. Have to tally last night's receipts and get the bank deposit in before noon and definitely before a few checks bounce."

"Sure," Theo said. "How about later. Maybe I'll head down to Bailey's for Irish coffee."

"Great!" Abby said, revving the Beemer. "See you then."

Theo headed up the walkway and did a quick one-eighty check around the courtyard patio. Satisfied that the gardener had done his job, she headed to her unit.

KC, her larger-than-life tabby, greeted her with "what's for dinner" in his cat-speak native tongue.

"Hi, boy! Let's get you some grub!"

After the cat condescended to accept lunch, she popped a Starbucks K-cup into her new Keurig and waited. Soon the aroma of fresh-brewed coffee filled the tiny kitchen. Leaning against the sink, cup in hand, Theo surveyed her tiny 1930s kitchen with its turquoise and black tile color scheme.

She inherited the *Las Casitas* courts from her grandmother. In the years since her grandmother's death, the steady income from its five units was what supported her through romantic breakups, job loss, and when work as a journalist didn't. With the exception of a microwave and her new Keurig, Theo kept it era-faithful, a tribute to the woman who raised her. This was Theo's home. Her tenants were good friends. Abby, Theo's best friend since fourth grade, was family.

Over the years, she'd had a few offers from developers who wanted to tear it down and build high-rise condominiums. She could have sold it and plumped up her bank account. As tempting as it might seem, selling the courts would have felt like a betrayal to her grandmother, her friends, but more importantly, to herself. She couldn't imagine living anywhere else.

At the computer, she scanned e-mails. Then she fired one off to Sam Morley.

"Finished your class assignment, Sam. I think you'll get some fresh recruits from the students. I told them what a sweetheart you were. Totally blew their minds since they were expecting *Spiderman's* J. Jonah Jameson from the *Daily Bugle*. As to more fiction, I told them you were a pussycat—always purring—never shouting. Bet your phone's ringing off the hook. You're welcome!" She hit "send" and waited. It didn't take long. As she expected, her cell phone erupted with *Darth Vader's* theme song—the one she assigned to Sam.

"Hi, Sam," she chirped.

"Don't 'Hi' me!" He barked. "What the hell? I need troupers, not spoiled pussies wanting their backs and egos massaged! Now I'll have break 'em in. Fine mess you've gotten me into, Theo!"

"Oh, Sam, calm down. I doubt if you'll get a single bite from this bunch. They were just interested in the gory stories. I doubt that these kids have the credentials or the stamina for hardline research. Of course, if you're planning to ditch print media for *Twitter* news feeds, then you just might have some takers."

"You're killing me here!" he groaned.

"Serves you right for dumping that stint on me!" Theo scolded.

"What? You'd rather do the social column assignments? Don't tempt me, Theo."

"Okay. Seriously. I handed out business cards to about twenty. Just about everyone took *The Tattlers*. So, who knows? You may get a good prospect outta this bunch yet."

"We'll see," he said.

There was a pause, then Sam asked, "Any word on Frank?"

"Nothing. Alex said she'd let me know."

Sam cleared his throat. "You'll let me know, right?"

"Right."

"Look, kiddo," Sam started in his fatherly advice tone, "Frank is smart and he's well-trained. Don't forget that. I think that guy is just doing his job. That's what I think."

"Thanks." The word caught in her throat.

She clicked off and shoved the phone in her pocket. Suddenly feeling very alone, she grabbed her hoodie and headed out the door for a walk.

Theo made her way to Hillcrest and cruised the boutiques. She must have walked fifteen blocks, meandering in and out of the small shops and mini-grocery stores. It was nearing three and her legs were beginning to feel like rubber. She hadn't eaten all day. At Mo's she ordered a hamburger to go and headed back home.

She ate half the burger, then offered a few morsels of meat to KC. He polished it off as if he were a starving stray. She fiddled around the house, straightening up, then took a hot shower. That helped. By four-thirty it was growing dark, thanks to daylight savings time. She figured she'd get to Bailey's for that Irish coffee before nightfall if she left now. Dressed for the chilly evening with rain in the forecast, she grabbed a heavy coat and an umbrella.

She didn't notice the manila envelope sticking partially out of her mailbox or the man in shadow sitting in his car in front of the complex.

3

Theo slid into the booth in the back, the one reserved for family, which she was as far as Abby was concerned. Abby saw her. Theo signaled "coffee" and, after refreshing the drinks of patrons at the bar, Abby poured two coffees, adding Canadian Club to Theo's, and made her way to the booth.

"Here ya go," Abby said, sliding the tall mug toward Theo. "Just what the doctor ordered."

"Thanks, doc!" Theo said, blowing into the brew and savoring the fumes before taking a sip.

"So, how'd you do at school?"

"Not bad. They were half-decent. They took some business cards and nearly all *The Tattlers*."

"Hankering for fast-food coupons no doubt."

"That's what I figure," Theo said, smirking.

"So," Abby started. "What's up?"

"What do you mean?"

"I *mean*, you have that 'we-need-to-talk' look. Seen it before. So, let's have it."

Theo cupped her hands around the mug and stared across the room at nothing in particular. "Oh . . . I don't know, Abs. I guess I'm just feeling . . . "

Abby reached across the table and gave Theo's hand a reassuring squeeze. "I know, sweetie. You've got to let it out, at least cry or something. You can't bottle this up inside. You're worried about Frank. Who wouldn't be? Just remember who and what he is. He's probably deep undercover and can't communicate. The guy's doing what he was trained to do."

Theo looked at her. "That's pretty much what Sam said."

"See. Fine minds and all that. Seriously, I have this gut feeling about the whole thing."

"I wish I could be so sure."

"Hey, you don't get to be sure. You're too close to this. Sam and me—hell, we have a different perspective. I'm telling you, sweetie, I think Frank is okay."

"Alex doesn't."

"Theo, Alex is too close, too. Like you—only *not* like you. If you get my drift. She's his 'work mother' so to speak. You're his lover. Either way, too close."

"Learn that at Psych-U, did you?"

"Hell, yeah. That and a lot of other useless hyperbole."

Theo nodded. "Thanks for that."

"Hey, you're welcome—and, no charge!"

Theo hung out at Bailey's for another hour. Hearing the laughter and banter of the regulars watching the various football games from anyone of the multiple flat screen TVs stuck to the walls, rooting for their favorite football teams, helped to take her mind off Frank a little. Around seven she left for home.

It was when she slid the key into the lock that she noticed the manila envelope jammed into the mailbox. There was no return address and no mailing address, only her name "Theo" written in a bold felt marker. The tiny hairs on her neck prickled as if someone just blew across them. She slipped inside and slid the deadbolt into place. She peered out the window but saw nothing other than a car's taillights turning the corner. She closed the shutters and turned her attention to the envelope.

Sliding the letter opener under the tab, she sliced it open and dumped the contents onto her desk: a half-sheet of paper wrapped around a small locket on a silver chain. Theo held the locket in her hand, then popped the clasp. There were two tiny photos. One she recognized immediately. It was of her as a baby. The other could have been a recent photo of her. Only, it wasn't. The hairstyle hadn't been current since the 1970s. It was a grainy snapshot of her mother.

Scrawled across the paper: "I know what happened to your mother. Meet me at the Old Mission at nine tonight."

A knock on her door startled her. "Yes?"

"Theo, it's me."

"Abs! Thank God!" she said, snapping the deadbolt.

"Hey, I got off early and thought you might want to talk, and . . . what's wrong? You look like you've seen a ghost."

Theo handed Abby the locket and the note.

Abby's eyes widened. "This is you—and this is your mother!"

Abby scanned the note, then glanced up. The look in her eyes said she wasn't buying it. "Who could have sent this? And why?"

"I don't know."

"Maybe it's a hoax. Maybe it's a trap. Maybe . . . "

"I have to find out."

"Shit! Of course, you do! Listen …," Abby grabbed her by the shoulders. "You don't know who sent this or how they got this locket. It could be some weirdo trying to lure you into a trap. It could even be a serial killer."

Theo was nodding. "I know."

Abby's eyes widened in disbelief. "You're *not* going?"

"What if . . . I mean, suppose it's her?" Theo stared at the tiny locket in her hand. "What if she's trying to reach out?"

"Of course. That's how all long-lost parents try to reconnect with their children; lure them to a deserted church after dark. Are you nuts! We should call the police."

Theo shook her head, "And tell them what?"

"Everything. You tell them the whole story. They just might conclude that your mother is, and I hate to say it, but . . . dead . . . and that it may be her killer trying to do to you whatever it was he did to your mother."

"I don't think so."

Abby shook her head, exasperated. "Fine! But I'm going with you! We'd better hurry, but first, I need to stop at my place."

They crossed the courtyard to Abby's unit. She dashed into the bedroom and returned with a handgun.

"You have a gun? Seriously, Abs!"

"Yeah. And I know how to use it. C'mon. I never thought I'd say this, but let's not be late to church."

They pulled into the parking lot of Mission de San Diego de Alcala a little before nine. There were still several cars in the old mission's parking lot and a few people were trickling out the door of the main building which was wide open and lit up.

Theo and Abby parked and headed inside.

"I didn't think they had Mass this late," Abby said as they settled into the last pew.

"I don't know if they do either. But I think they still do novenas and benedictions," Theo whispered.

"Oh. Yeah," Abby said, nodding and thinking she hadn't done a benediction in decades, let alone committed to the nine days of prayer required for a bona-fide *novena*.

The church emptied quickly and before long they were the only two left. An acolyte extinguished the candles on the altar as the priest dimmed the main lights, darkening the nave to shadow. Only the sanctuary light remained, glowing red across the altar, then disappearing into the dark.

Theo watched the ritual, remembering its significance in Catholic liturgy and feeling a tiny jab of conscience. The light symbolized Christ's presence in the Tabernacle—a comforting thought. In the darkened church waiting for the mystery man—or woman—to show up, Theo hoped it wasn't just an old wives' tale.

The priest turned in their direction and nodded. Theo figured he was anxious to lock up, but was giving them a few minutes to complete their devotions. Abby slipped onto her knees, leaned her elbows onto the backrest of the pew in front of them, and bowed her head as if in prayer—buying them some time.

They waited.

A few minutes later, they figured he or she wasn't coming. Theo motioned to Abby to leave.

"Well, that was a bust!" Abby said as they started down the well-worn steps. Theo grabbed Abby's arm and nodded toward the figure leaning against a car parked next to theirs. When he turned toward them, Theo recognized him immediately. He was the bearded man who had been staring at her in the university elevator. "I saw this guy earlier today," she whispered.

The figure turned toward them. "We can talk inside," he said. The door locks popped and he motioned to them to get in. Abby's hand slid into her coat pocket and rested on the butt of her gun. Theo and Abby approached the man's late-model Mercedes sedan. Theo shook her head. "Sorry, but I don't know you."

"No, you don't. Let me introduce myself. My name is Tafiq Ibrahim, *Professor* Ibrahim from the university. I knew your mother. I'm not a serial killer. But what I have to say is very private. Now, join me in the car, please. Your friend may sit in the back seat. I'm certain the gun she has in her pocket is cocked and can be fired within a nano-second. You, young lady, have the advantage."

Ibrahim slid his seat back so he could face Theo without craning his neck. He smiled. "You look just like her, you know. That is why I stared at you today. For a moment . . . I thought … I hoped …" His words trailed off as he looked away.

"How do you have this?" Theo held out the locket.

"It was a long time ago, Theo. In San Francisco. Your mother and my brother Ahmed were . . . close. You see, your father had been killed in the war. Your mother came to San Francisco to tend to her mother, who was dying. After her mother died, she was distraught. My brother and I had lost family members. He, too, was suffering from grief. It is, how can I say this so you can understand. It is a hole cut in your heart. I don't think it ever heals."

Theo nodded. "I know."

"Ah, Theo. I suspect you do. I think you feel the pain of losing someone dear. Am I right?"

Theo stopped short of mentioning Frank. She leveled her gaze, "So what's this about?"

"My brother and your mother met at a grief counseling session. Over a few weeks they became friends. I think they answered each other's cry for help. Eventually, they became more than that."

"Your brother and my mother were lovers?"

He nodded. "My brother and I were close. He told me that he was in love with Dena, that her husband had been killed in the war and that she had a daughter. He said she spoke of you often. She planned to bring you to San Francisco. Then . . . then, their world collapsed."

"She died?"

Ibrahim shook his head. "I thought so . . . at first." He looked away. "Now . . . I'm not so sure. Let me start at the beginning.

"You have to understand, Theo, they were young. Ahmed had been an engineering student in Paris. He was doing postgraduate work at Berkeley. It was the tail end of the Vietnam War. Conflicts in our homeland, Palestine, left many, including our family, dead. Ahmed and I were all that was left. You can understand. We were angry. We fit right into the spirit of unrest. Young people all over America were angry—your mother about the senseless war and losing your father; Ahmed about the loss of our homeland and family. I think they wanted to fight back against the injustices.

"Ahmed confided in me. He said that he and Dena joined a group of fellow students who wanted to change the politics that supported the war. They staged protests. They marched. Then, Ahmed fell into a deeper cell of activism—it turned deadly. Your mother worked at Congressman Jack O'Keefe's re-election campaign office. O'Keefe was a key player in Washington and had pushed for the government to side with Israel against Palestine. He really worked for a conglomerate that wanted to control oil rights in the Mideast. Just one more of the elite who spewed sanctimonious rhetoric while they lined their pockets with gold at the cost of innocent lives!"

Ibrahim turned away. After a moment, he looked at Theo. "I'm sorry. It's just that nothing has changed in decades. I doubt if it ever will."

Theo studied him, waited, then she said, "What happened?"

Ibrahim faced her. "They thought they could infiltrate O'Keefe's operation. I think they hoped they could expose his scheme."

"Did they?"

"Yes . . . and no. The group of dissidents had a terrorist cell that Ahmed didn't know about. This cell planned to bomb O'Keefe's headquarters and kill him. That was never Ahmed's plan—not his and certainly not your mother's. But it happened despite their efforts to stop it."

Abby chirped up, "I remember reading about that a long time ago. Some of O'Keefe's staff were killed, but he wasn't there that day."

"That's right," Ibrahim said. "He escaped. But the others did not."

"Did my mother die?"

"And that's the question, isn't it? I thought she did. She would have been the only woman in the office that day. And there was a body—a woman—badly burned. The authorities *presumed* it was her. I had hoped that maybe she escaped and went into hiding. Ahmed managed to get out of the country. He went to Italy."

"Did he ever try to contact you—or her?"

"No. We lost touch. Then, years later, I learned through sources that he had returned to Palestine, joined a resistance group and died there."

"Why are you trying to find my mother?"

"Closure. If she escaped the bombing, I need to know. You see, Theo, Ahmed told me that she was pregnant with their child. If she is alive, I must find my only living relative. If she is dead," he looked away, "if that is the truth, then I will mourn her and my brother's unborn child."

"Why wouldn't she have come forward if she's alive? Why wouldn't she have tried to contact Ahmed or you?"

"That's the question, isn't it?" Ibrahim was staring at her. Then he leaned toward her.

"Do you ever trust your gut, Theo?"

He didn't wait for a response.

"Yes. I'm certain you do. The gut doesn't lie. My gut tells me that she never got inside that building. Maybe she got close to the door. She could have been just outside when the bomb went off. Maybe she was thrown to the ground, hit her head and was knocked unconscious — perhaps she was seriously injured. She could have had amnesia and didn't know, or remember, who she was.

"Ahmed said he tried to find out if she survived. Then the news hit the airwaves. They said a woman in the office was killed. In one swift moment he'd lost her and their child. That's what he believed, you see. That's why he left."

"But you — rather your gut — doesn't believe she died."

Ibrahim shook his head. "I don't. Not at all. After he died, I, too, lost everything. All I had was an old photo of her in that locket that Ahmed had sent me. I put it away. Closed the door, so to speak. I had given up hope . . . then, today, I saw you."

"What did you think? That I knew if she was alive?"

"No, my dear Theo. The moment I saw you I believed it was a sign. I immediately did what research I could to find out who you were. I have a trusted researcher—a former student—who helped. Within a few short hours I pretty much knew everything about you."

"Seriously?"

"Yes, most definitely. You look so much like her, you know. And your work history—your campaigns—you have her same urgency to do what is right. You even . . . " he reached his hand out and moved her hair back.

"I'm right here, Ibrahim," Abby spoke up.

"I'm so sorry, I didn't mean to . . . I simply couldn't help myself, Theo."

"No offense to your gut, but what is it that you want from me?"

Ibrahim smiled and shook his head. "Nothing, my dear. Only to give you that locket. And, to tell you what I knew about your mother and my brother and to say . . . "

"What? That she was dumb enough to be involved in a terrorist cell that killed innocent people?"

Ibrahim sighed. "And there it is. Youth—you are all so judgmental. You jump like a hair-trigger. We were like that once. But, no, my dear Theo. That's not what I want to tell you. If your mother is dead, then you should know that she didn't desert you—not on purpose."

"And if she's alive? What excuse can you give me then?"

Ibrahim shook his head. "I can't explain that. I can only guess that fear played a part in her disappearance. Fear of being judged guilty. Fear of being silenced by the real terrorists. What I can tell you, Theo, is that I truly do not blame you for the fury of a raw temper. I understand that it is the result of a deep hurt. I only hope that in your heart you can forgive her. I thought that my information would close the door on the pain that you have suffered. But, if you are led to try to find her, I want to help. If she survived, then I can only hope my brother's child did, too."

Theo rested her hand on the door handle. "Thank you for this information and for returning this locket to me."

The door swung open and she was out of the car and heading toward her own.

"Young woman," Ibrahim said, turning toward Abby. "As her good friend, you must help her. She will be angry for some time. Believe me, I understand." He handed her his card. "If she wants to talk to me, or if you do, get in touch. I owe it to her—and to her mother."

4

San Francisco – 1977

He sat so he could see her and the group leader. He didn't want to appear as if he was staring at her, but the young, auburn-haired woman was beautiful. He couldn't not look at her. He'd only heard about "love at first sight" as an American idiom. Until now, he thought it stupidly romantic, an affectation of the foolish and self-centered. A man such as himself, with the weight of tragedy and loss that he had endured most of his life in his native Palestine, would never be so stupid as to fall for such silliness.

Romance was a dalliance of the insipid with too much time on their hands and no war to wage. But this woman caught his interest—from her long, shapely legs, crossed demurely at the ankles, to her middle-class moral innocence lacking sophistication—so totally American. He was unabashedly captivated. The fact that she had a lovely face with movie-star qualities made it easy. He allowed himself the diversion. It would be brief. Love was not on his timetable. Lust, on the other hand, was.

"Ahmed, have you anything to add?" the group leader asked.

Ahmed cleared his throat. He hadn't been paying attention to the comments of the large woman talking about her dead husband. She bored him, as did the entire grief-counseling group therapy exercise. He had only joined because he had to write a paper for his psychology class on grief and its processing. He didn't even like psychology. He saw it as a ridiculous waste of time for an engineering major. Another idiotic American habit of pandering to the emotional and not enough emphasis on real-world practicality.

He could see the counselor and the rest of the group expected a response. He gave them one. "In our hearts, we all feel the depth of your suffering," he said with solemnity and elegance.

The woman gasped and sobbed. Ahmed winced, thinking he had made a serious gaffe. Then, she put her hands to her face and blubbered, "Oh, thank you, Ahmed!" She looked around the circle. "Thank you all for understanding my pain."

Hankies were produced and dabbed at eight pairs of eyes—all but Ahmed's and the auburn-haired woman's.

Ahmed's eyes caught hers. A twitch at the corner of her mouth as if she were stifling a laugh made it clear that she was onto him. He felt a flutter of excitement. He intended to pursue it, wherever it led.

By the time their group had completed its six-week stint, Ahmed had taken Dena to coffee three times, to a movie (*Rocky*), a concert (Wings), and to bed. Within a few short weeks, she had told him how her husband, an Air Force pilot, was shot down in 1975 during the evacuation of civilians from Saigon. He listened as she vented her frustrations over the government's meddling in Southeast Asia. He sympathized at her rage at the loss of over 58,000 American servicemen during the Vietnam War. He consoled her when she wept, condemning God for the injustice of innocent deaths. He gained her trust. He introduced her to his fellow dissidents—students who had protested the war and now turned to rallying against growing environmental issues, civil rights, and political corruption from the presidency down, brought to light with the Watergate scandal.

In the ensuing weeks, Ahmed gained her confidence and trust. He kept any conversation about his past light, highlighting the art and romance of the exotic world of the Middle East. He did not talk about the dark side, about his losses. He took his time, only introducing Dena to the philosophical and humanitarian aspects of dangerous world politics when he believed she was ready. To accept his involvement in active underground movements, she would have to trust—and love—him. Eventually, he had not only won over a convert, but had made strides toward striking a lethal blow to a high-ranking U.S. congressman, a key figure in the Israel-Palestine peace talks. Ahmed's plan was nearing ground zero. Dena would play a crucial part in it.

Dena sat at the table in a corner of Caffé Trieste on Vallejo Street in North Beach. Now a paying customer, she recalled her days working behind the counter, waiting tables, and depending on tips to make ends meet. Sal and Rosa Crivello, the owners, gave her a job when they really didn't need another employee. It was simple. They had a soft spot for Dena, the young widow, struggling to pay her mother's debts and earn a living while she planned to bring her baby daughter to San Francisco to be with her. They were decent like that.

"Dena! How's it going," Sal yelled over the whooshing of the cappuccino machine as he filled a cup with frothy milk. "Running for Congress yet?"

Dena smiled and waved. "Not a chance, Sal! How about you?"

Sal chuckled and waved off the running joke.

Dena felt at home there. The owners, employees, and patrons meshed together like a big, happy, quarrelsome family. It was the ambience, the old-world allure, that welcomed her just as it had so many others.

For Dena, San Francisco was not just an icon, a beacon of new movements and ideas, it was a dream for the future after the nightmares of the past.

In the tiny North Beach community, Caffé Trieste was a microcosm of San Francisco's allure. It embodied the mood and character of the people. It was a refuge of hope. At its well-worn wooden tables, with mismatched chairs, patrons enjoyed the ambience—the smells and sounds, the gurgle and whoosh of espresso machines pumping out the rich, dark essence of caffeine and frothy cappuccinos. The sweet fragrance of anise in freshly baked biscotti and other Italian pastries perfumed the air. The murmur of patrons' voices mingled with playful banter and laughter.

These were the sights, sounds and smells of a safe haven for ideas. Here they could talk freely about changing the government's world-view mind-set. Dena, and her hope for a better future for herself and for her daughter, fit right in.

It was where she and Ahmed had their first "coffee date." Over the few quick weeks that she had come to know and love Ahmed Ibrahim, she embraced his ideals as willingly and as easily as she had fallen for him. It was with Ahmed's scheme at the forefront of her plans for the future that she felt confident to write Mary Catherine Hunter, her former mother-in-law, and lay out her plan:

Dear Mom, it's been so difficult coming to terms with myself. After Jim's death and then my mother's, I didn't know what to do. I fell apart. These past few weeks as I rummaged through mother's belongings and settled her estate, I could barely hold my head above water—financially and emotionally. That's an odd way of putting it. Funny, because more than once I found myself sitting on the wall above the rocky shore near the bridge where Jim and I used to sit and talk for hours. It was that same view—the happy one, filled with hope and promise of our future—that was now a bleak reminder of what I once had and could never have again.

Often, as I sat looking out at the grey seas, I fought the urge not to go on. I wanted to put an end to the emptiness inside. The only saving thought during those terrible dark days was of little Theo. I could never leave her. I love her and miss her so.

I managed to get through that awful time. I got counseling and started to heal. It was during the healing that I realized how much I missed home—San Francisco. San Diego will be where I have wonderful memories of my time with you and Jim before he left for Vietnam. But San Francisco will always be home.

I've found a nice apartment in North Beach. I've gotten an office job. I'm getting back on my feet. I want to get established first, then I plan to bring Theo here. That may take another couple of months and I hope that isn't a problem for you.

Of course, Theo and I will visit you in San Diego often, especially for the holidays. I can't imagine not being with you and Theo at Christmas. You two are the whole of my family now. I don't know what I would have done without you, Mom. In the midst of your own grieving for Jim, you found the strength to comfort me. You treated me as a daughter. I will be ever grateful to you for that.

I don't have a phone right now. I'm saving money for a deposit so I can establish an account in my name. As soon as I have one, I'll call you. In the meantime, you can write me in care of the Post Office. I pick up my mail regularly.

Please hug my darling baby and tell her we'll be together soon.

With love,
Dena

Dena folded the letter and slipped it into the envelope. She sealed it and put it in her purse intending to mail it the next morning.

Just around 2 p.m. Dena was headed to her job at Congressman Jack O'Keefe's office. Before she got to the building's front door, the bomb went off. Much of the interior of the office was destroyed. Two staff members died. Only Dena survived. She never made it into the building and was found unconscious outside on the street. Workers from nearby offices and residents from an apartment building came to her aid and stayed with her until the ambulance arrived. None claimed to know her. It was believed she was simply a passerby who was caught in the blast. Her purse with her identification disappeared.

Dena was rushed to St. Francis Memorial Hospital, where she lay in a coma for days. When she awoke, she had amnesia.

When the investigators sifted through the debris, they only found employment records identifying two staff members—a man and a woman. Dena had used her maiden name "Dena Hartsohn," when she was hired. Other than her San Francisco address, she listed no next of kin.

The woman's body was so badly burned and mangled that a positive identification was impossible. The medical examiner declared that the young woman killed in the blast was the female employee—Dena Hartsohn.

All connection to Dena's previous life was severed—including her relationships in San Diego to her mother-in-law and baby daughter. The letter to Mary Catherine Hunter was never mailed.

With no identification and no memory, Dena Hartsohn became "Jane Doe." After a few weeks with no improvement in her memory, she was sent to a convalescent hospital in Marin County. Dena Hartsohn Hunter was never heard from again.

5

Present Day – San Diego

Theo turned the key in the padlock and pulled up the door on the garage. There was her grandmother's bedframe with its head and footboards, and a cabinet that held a complete set of Christmas china—something Theo kept, but never used. There were a few boxes marked "Xmas," which Theo knew held her grandmother's tree ornaments, a Nativity set, and every photo Christmas card they'd ever received.

Next to these sat more boxes—stacks and stacks of them. These held rental receipts, legal documents and other files that her grandmother had kept throughout her years as owner of the *Las Casitas* cottages. Theo had avoided going through them. Until now, there hadn't been a reason to do so. Now, there was an urgency to find anything that might give her a clue to her mother's life in San Francisco.

Systematically, she opened each box and sifted through tenant files, receipts, and tax records. Grandmother Catherine had been thorough and, it appeared, didn't toss a thing! Over her 30 years ownership of the rentals, she had kept everything (and anything) related to her tenants.

Theo figured she could dispose of seventy-five percent of the files. Yet, she didn't want to. They were memories of her grandmother—even her thoroughness in recordkeeping was important as a way of preserving her memory. After box eleven, Theo felt as if her eyes would cross if she had to read another file. Then, she found the box marked "Jim." She popped the lid.

James Hunter's military service was summed up simply. His Air Force service record, certificates of merit, assignments and other documents were in a manila envelope suitably marked. Beneath the envelope rested a neatly, tri-corner-folded American flag (the one that had draped his coffin), and a black velvet box. Theo opened the box and stared at the gold five-pointed star, encircled by a crown of laurel and oak on a green background. The center of the star contained the bas relief of the head of the Statue of Liberty. The star was suspended from a bar inscribed with the word "VALOR" above the thunderbolt insignia from the Air Force Coat of Arms. The medal was attached to a light blue moiré silk ribbon with a center chevron containing thirteen white stars. It was the Medal of Honor, the highest award that can be conferred by the United States government on its military for personal acts of valor above and beyond the call of duty.

There was a newspaper clipping and a black and white photograph of Theo's grandmother and Dena holding three-year old Theo's hand as President Carter presented her with the commendation. Written below the photo:

"Presented on this day, February 1, 1977, to Lt. James Thomas Hunter, USAF, for his extraordinary heroism on April 30, 1975. Lt. Hunter was mortally wounded in action during Operation Frequent Wind on April 30, 1975. Accepting the posthumous award were his mother, Mary Catherine; his wife, Dena; and his daughter Theodosia."

A citation accompanying the Medal read: "On behalf of a Grateful Nation, we present this, our highest honor, to Lt. James Thomas Hunter, USAF, for valor under fire during the rescue of military personnel and civilians on

April 30, 1975." It was signed, "James Earl Carter, Jr., President of the United States of America."

Theo knew the story. During Operation Frequent Wind, the evacuation of South Vietnamese and U.S. and foreign nationals on April 30, 1975, Hunter's helicopter had been fired upon by the North Vietnamese ground forces during the capture of Saigon as he lifted off, loaded with U.S. Embassy personnel, and Vietnamese men, women, and children. Although he was gravely wounded, he had gallantly delivered his precious cargo to the waiting USS Kirk patrolling off the coast at Vung Tau, near the mouth of the Saigon River. He died, still strapped into his harness.

She stared at the photo and the medal. Her father had been a hero. She never knew him.

Another thought leapt at her—this was about Frank and whether she might soon be holding another medal conferred by the government. This one for an FBI agent killed in the line of duty.

Suddenly, Theo couldn't catch her breath. She pulled herself up and stumbled to the door, desperately gulping for air. She fumbled in her pocket for her inhaler which, miraculously, she had had the foresight to bring with her, thinking that the stale air in the closed-up garage might trigger her asthma. This, she knew, wasn't asthma. It was a panic attack—the result of her lungs being paralyzed with fear.

The inhaler helped and within moments she was taking in air. There was something else. She was accepting the fact that Frank was dead. That hit her like a gut-punch. She slid down the doorjamb, hugging her stomach as if she could somehow stop the pain. The sobbing came next.

Grief is a personal road, traveled alone. In that little corner of the backyard, bracing herself against the garage lintel, Theo was coming to terms with hers. When there were no more tears to be shed, Theo picked herself up, dusted the caked dirt off the knees of her jeans, and headed back inside.

Theo closed the box containing the remnants of her father's history and his life. Crouching, she shoved it back into its place among the other discarded reminders of her family history.

Her legs cramped and her back hurt. She stood, stretched and was reaching for the light switch when she glimpsed another box jammed in behind the tenant records. She hadn't noticed it before. The lid had become crushed by the weight of the stacked boxes on top of it. She jostled it out from under them and read the partially faded scribble on what was left of the lid. "Hunter." She peeled away the remnant of sealing tape and opened it. There were packets of letters and old photographs.

She bundled this box under her arm and headed out of the garage, securing the lock.

"Hey!" Abby called from the porch of Theo's unit. "I was wondering where you were. You left your door unlocked and … Jeezus! You look like you saw a ghost! You okay?"

"I was … just looking through the garage. Found this," she said, holding out the box.

"Where's your inhaler? There's probably old insecticide and god knows what other toxic shit in there. Did it bring on your asthma? Come on, let's get you out into the air."

"I'm okay," Theo mumbled. "I just want to go inside."

Abby took the box and slid her arm around Theo. Inside, Theo sat on the couch and stared at the box, not touching it. Abby handed her a glass of ice water and settled beside her. "Wanna talk?"

"In a minute."

It took a few minutes before the color crept back into her face. She gulped some water, then set the glass aside. She pulled the box onto her lap and rifled through it.

"Photos!" Abby was excited. "Let's see what you've got here."

They started sifting through photos. Many were taken in the '30s and '40s and were of Theo's grandmother.

"I was hoping we'd see what your grandfather looked like. I don't see any men in these photos that might have been him," Abby said.

"Grams never talked about him. I just figured either she left him and moved to California when my dad was little. Or, maybe she was never married. I figured he just wasn't anyone she wanted in the picture."

"Yeah," Abby mumbled. "Probably a serial killer or something."

"Given my family history, I wouldn't doubt it," Theo said, sounding as if she believed it.

"Hey, look here," Abby said, holding a small bundle of envelopes. "These are from your dad to your grandmother."

Theo grabbed them and discarded the rubber band that all but crumbled in her fingers. She sifted through the bundle. There were six with a military return address:

Lt. J. T. Hunter, 0-1326344,
H1, MACV (PIO),
APO San Francisco, Calif., 96243

"If he wrote to my mother, and I can't believe he didn't, then she must not have lived here. She must have been living in San Francisco at the time. What I need is her address."

Abby scanned her bundle and reported her findings.

"Pretty standard fare. Just reassuring her that he was eating well and safe. Looks like he was in San Francisco waiting for orders to ship out. No mention of where he was going, though. Guess he didn't want to worry her. Oh, wait a minute. Listen to this. He says the usual … 'food's good … getting plenty of rest … shipping out soon but won't be in danger …' oh, then he says, 'I've met someone. She's a local. She works at a coffee shop. She's beautiful, funny and wants to meet you, mom. You'll love her…' Wow! Talk about the sandwich effect."

"Let me see that," Theo said, snatching the letter.

"Damn! No indication of where she lived. He might not even be talking about her. Could be some other girl he met."

Theo pulled the snapshots from the box and set them aside. Underneath was another bundle of envelopes—fifteen in all. These were all addressed to her grandmother with no return address and with different postmarks, cities up and down the coast: Richmond, San Rafael, Novato, Vallejo, Oakland, Hayward, Mountain View, San Jose, Fremont, Watsonville, Santa Cruz, etc. They were dated from 1979 through 1994—fifteen years' worth.

Inside each was a postal money order receipt for $300. The receipts totaled over $4,500.

"Abby, what do you make of this?"

Abby scoured the envelopes. "Someone sent your grandmother $300 every year for fifteen years. Who would do that—and why?"

"It's obvious, isn't it," Theo said. "This is child support. For me. From my mother. What else *could* it be?"

"That's not a lot of money to raise a kid," Abby said.

"With Dena out of the picture, I was my dad's sole surviving dependent. Grams received my dad's military survivor benefits for me. Not that it was a whole hell of a lot of money. I'm guessing this is just something additional that Dena sent. Probably trying to soothe her guilty conscience."

"That means that your grandmother knew Dena was alive."

"Why wouldn't she tell me that? All these years . . . I just assumed she . . . "

"Maybe your grandmother knew Dena was involved in that bombing. Maybe she had to keep it secret to protect her . . . and you. But, more importantly, Ibrahim was right." Abby said. "She survived that bombing. At least you know she was still alive in 1994. But why stop in 1994?"

"That's the year Grams died. Dena stopped because she couldn't let me know. She was in hiding all those years. Grams knew it. When Grams died, so did Dena's connection to me."

Abby riffled through the envelopes. "She should have sent you a message, Theo."

"You'd think so, wouldn't you?"

"Maybe she just couldn't chance it. Maybe she kept tabs on you some other way."

"Do you think she hired a private detective to check up on me, then report back to her? I doubt that. I think she sent Grams money for my support. By the time Grams died, she figured I was on my own and didn't need the money."

"Seems a little cold, doesn't it?"

Theo let out a dry cough of a laugh without a trace of humor. "Totally in character, don't you think?"

"That's a little harsh, even for you," Abby said.

"Okay, so much for sentimental musings. Here's what this says. One, Dena didn't die in that explosion, even though it was believed she was one of the victims. Two, someone else died in her place. Three, she went into hiding—for fifteen years. Four, she sent money to Grams for my care. Five, she stopped when Grams died. Six, I don't have a six. That's where my imagining stops."

"Do you think she's still alive?" Abby asked.

"Should I care?" Theo said, tossing the envelopes back into the box. She got up and headed over to the sink and started washing the breakfast cups and dishes.

Abby said nothing. She picked up the envelopes and laid them in a pile. Then she gathered the photos and started going through them, sorting them by date. Theo watched in the reflection of the window above the sink. Abby picked up a notepad and made a few scribbles. Theo said nothing. She washed down the counter and rearranged a few decorative items on the shelves that flanked the kitchen window.

"When you're done stalling in there," Abby said, "you could help me."

"Help you what?"

Abby glanced at Theo over the rims of her glasses. "I'll bet your mother is still alive. I'll even bet that she was hoping one day you'd find these envelopes and put two and two together."

"Two-and-two? As in she washed her hands of me and tried to ease her conscience by sending money to Grams for a few years? As in, when Grams died, then poof! She vanished?"

"I swear, Theo! You have the hardest head! No! That's not the equation and you know it! Your mother was in trouble—big trouble. She went into hiding and couldn't resurface. Maybe because that would have put you and your grandmother in danger. So, she does the only thing she can. She sends money to your grandmother to let her know she's still alive and that she still cares. Your grandmother—a much smarter and, apparently, far more intuitive person than you—*gets* it. She saves the proof in the hope that someday she can talk to you about it. Unfortunately, she died before she could."

"That's not an equation. That's a theory. Big difference in probability."

Abby groaned. "Could you just stop being a jerk for two seconds and think about it?"

"I have thought about it. Look, Abs, even if what you've said is true, what do you want me to do?"

Abby walked over to her, took her by the shoulders and gave her a squeeze. "What I want you to do is to consider that your mother is still alive and that you have an obligation to try to find her. I think she's hoping you will."

"You, of all people, want me to launch an investigation into my mother's whereabouts?

"You do realize that, if what you purport is true, it's likely that she's been in hiding because she's guilty. If she surfaces, someone somewhere might recognize her and put two and two together. If the FBI is alerted—and they most certainly would be—then, she'd be apprehended. If tried, she'd probably get the death penalty or go to prison for the rest of her life.

"And, if all that is true, then there may be accomplices who, like her, have been in hiding all these years. I'm guessing they'd rather kill her than take a chance that she'd expose them. They're not likely to want to put their own necks on the chopping block.

"If I find her—an astronomical big 'if'—I could put both of us in danger? And *this* is what you want me to do?"

"Yep."

Theo shook her head. "Impossible. You. Of all people. Don't you have a list of how many times you lectured—no—*scolded* me—for getting entangled in my investigative work?"

Abby shrugged. "So?"

Theo shook her head. "So? So why is this any different?"

"Because she's your mother. Because you need closure," Abby said as though it were the only possible rational conclusion.

"Look, Theo," she said, pointing to the photos. "In this pile we have your mom and dad together, hanging out in San Francisco. Standard tourist shots. But these," she pointed to a second stack of photos. "Neighborhood shots. This is where they lived. These places could still be there. Maybe, just maybe, you could show these photos around. Maybe someone would remember her."

"Uh huh, and then what?"

"It could lead to a clue," Abby said.

"And from there?"

"Oh, I don't know. You're the investigative snoop. I'm thinking you might figure out where they lived. Maybe someone is still around who knew them. And, then—"

"Abby" Theo cut in. "It's unlikely I'll find anybody who's still living in the area that would remember my mother. Damn near impossible, actually."

"All I'm saying is think about it. I'm sure your investigative brain will figure something out. Even if you strike a big zero, personally, I think walking in her footsteps would do you a world of good."

"I don't."

"Theo, look at these. Please," Abby said, handing her a stack of photos.

Theo let out an exaggerated groan and took them. She leafed through the candid shots of San Francisco landmarks. "Nothing," Theo said, tossing them back into the box.

"I must have lucked out," Abby said, holding up several snapshots. All were of the same handsome couple standing in the forefront with famous tourist haunts in the background: Fisherman's Wharf, the Golden Gate Bridge, waving from the cable car with Lombard Street to the right, Ghirardelli Square, a coffee shop.

"Wait a second," Theo said, grabbling the photo of the coffee shop. "He said she worked at a coffee shop. What's the name, can you read that sign?"

Abby grabbed the magnifying glass and scrunched her eyes. "No, but look at that!" She was pointing to a street sign just off the side. The sign read, "Vallejo St."

Theo Googled a San Francisco street map and located Vallejo Street in North Beach. She used the satellite view to give her a street view. That yielded three cafés. She Googled each name and found that only one of them was in existence in the seventies—*Caffé Trieste.*

"God bless Google!" Abby yelped in excitement.

Theo was skeptical. "You think she worked there? Even if she did, that was over thirty years ago, nearly forty. You think anybody's still around who knew her or my father?"

"I don't know, Theo. What else do you have to go on? It's worth a try. Suppose you discover the real Dena—not the child deserter or terrorist—don't you want to know something good about her? Your grandmother protected her. That's got to mean something. Besides, you need a road trip."

Theo stared at the happy shining faces of her mom and dad, full of hope for their future and looking out at the camera as if they had the rest of their lives just waiting for them. She felt a twinge of conscience. There was no ignoring the nagging weight of the burden to prove that the woman he had loved, the one her grandmother had trusted and protected, wasn't a monster.

"Okay. I'll go—if you go with me!"

Abby winced, "Damn! I've got the IRS snoops chewing on my books for the next few days. I'd love to leave them flopping in the wind, but I don't dare. I'm the only one who can explain why my dry-cleaning bill for T-shirts and jeans are bona fide deductibles."

Theo looked skeptical. Abby explained. "I don't provide uniforms for myself or my employees. Do you have any idea how many drunks spill drinks? Not just on the table, but on the servers? So, I pay their cleaning bills. It's a business expense. Deductible. Get it?"

Theo did. It made sense. "I get it. Will the IRS?"

"We'll see. But I have to be there to explain that and other things.

"So, I can't go, but I think you need someone with you. How about Ibrahim?"

Theo looked skeptical. "Do *you* trust him?"

Abby shook her head. "Not really."

"Fine. I'm tired of listening to you. If I don't go, you'll never shut up about it. I think I can do a little sleuthing in San Francisco on my own."

"You're going to contact Congressman O'Keefe, too, aren't you?"

Theo thought a moment. "That might be a possibility. But what records would he have? According to the news reports his office was destroyed. Besides, he's retired. What could he know—or even remember? I don't think I'll be digging up any of that old dirt. I'll just focus on tracing my mother's life before all that."

Abby stared at the photos. "You'll be careful?"

"I'm always careful," Theo quipped.

Abby's eyes widened. "You need a partner."

"You can't go, Abs. And, seriously, it's just for a day. Two at the most. I can almost bet this is barking up a dead tree."

"Mixed metaphors aside, you watch it!"

"Don't worry. I will."

"Say," Abby said, "wanna take my gun?"

Theo's look could have melted Antarctica.

"I guess that's a 'no,' huh?"

6

Ibrahim sat behind his desk and pressed his fingers together. He closed his eyes. The student shifted uncomfortably in his seat unsure whether the professor was thinking over his answer, or if he'd simply fallen asleep. The young man cleared his throat.

"Professor?" he all but whispered.

Getting no response, he repeated the question a little louder. "Professor?"

Ibrahim shifted slightly in his chair. Without opening his eyes, he said, "Tell me, Mr. Booth, in your opinion, what personal characteristics do you feel are necessary to be a successful design engineer?"

Booth was stunned. This was not what he expected. He'd scheduled the appointment with the professor regarding clarification he needed concerning a class assignment. He thought that the professor might not understand that.

"Professor Ibrahim, I really don't think . . . "

Ibrahim interrupted. "You see, Booth, that's the problem."

"Sir?"

Ibrahim tapped his forehead with two fingers—"You don't think."

Booth's cheeks flamed. He pulled on his collar as though the room was heating up—closing in.

"Pardon me, sir?" he said, swiping his sleeve across his forehead glistening wet with perspiration.

"You have an *'ah-sign-ment'*," Ibrahim said slowly, enunciating each syllable. It is up to you to determine how to approach solving the problem presented. It is not up to me to interpret—neither the spoken nor the written word. Do you think your clients will interpret their wants for you? No. Do you think they will sit down with you and go over every detail of the job? No. They will tell you they want lots of light, or lots of room. They tell you how they need space to practice the violin or the piano, or dab hue and tint to canvas, or to write. They will not tell you how to create a room that squeezes out those creative juices so that they may create the perfect symphony, paint the next Mona Lisa, or pen the next great American novel.

"They will only tell you if you have succeeded into creating a space that *doesn't* inspire them—or they simply won't pay you. Thus, it is *you*, my dear Booth, who interprets their wants and validates them. That's how it's done, you see. That's your task.

"I trust I am clear. Now, go. Take my demands and build me a model. Dismissed," he said, waving his hand contemptuously. "Scoot."

With that, the student rose and trod quietly out of the room and past the line of other students waiting outside the door.

"Next!" Ibrahim's voice bellowed out into the hall.

Kasim Jabul waited until the professor's afternoon appointment time had ended. He watched amused as each student had his or her fifteen minutes of torture with Ibrahim. He was even more entertained by the looks of frustration, fear, or simple confusion on their faces after their "counseling" sessions. He remembered his first encounter and his own muddle after the professor's little pep talk. Now, a graduate student, he had come to appreciate the professor's directness and his skill at teaching students the art of self-appraisal and problem-solving.

"Kasim?" Ibrahim roared from his office. "Are you out there?"

Kasim walked leisurely into Ibrahim's office and slipped effortlessly into the chair facing the desk. He stretched his long legs out in front and crossed them.

"You scare the shit out of them, you know," Kasim said, smiling.

"Yes. I do, don't I," Ibrahim laughed. "Isn't it fun!"

"It's a wonder any of them stay in the program," Kasim added.

"They must learn not to expect everything to be handed to them. They must earn respect. Most of these young people have not had to struggle for anything. They are spoiled. My job is not to be their wet nurse."

"That, sir, you surely are not!" Kasim laughed.

Ibrahim left his position of authority behind the desk and moved to the chair next to Kasim.

"I have a job for you. It involves the young woman whom you did the research on."

Ibrahim explained the circumstances and told Kasim that he wanted him to follow Theo around and report back to him on what she uncovers.

"You want me to get her to trust me."

"Yes. You're quite good at that. I trust you and I don't trust many."

Kasim nodded. "Will I get a formal introduction to her? Or shall I simply surprise her?"

"I'm not certain she trusts me completely yet. I'm about to find out."

Ibrahim dialed Theo's cell phone. She picked up almost immediately.

"Theo, this is Professor Ibrahim. How are you, my dear?"

Theo sounded surprised and hesitant. "I'd ask how you got my number, but something tells me that would be academic."

"Well, I am very good at research, which is why I'm calling you. Do you recall when we met that I mentioned my student who was able to locate you? He, too, is an excellent researcher. And that, my dear, is why I'm calling."

"To tell me that I can run but I can't hide?"

Ibrahim laughed. "No. No. Definitely not. I want to offer my researcher's assistance. I suspect you could use some help. He comes with no strings. He is trustworthy and he is honest. What do you say, my dear?"

"No. Thank you."

"I see. Do you mind if I ask why a talented and seasoned investigative journalist, such as yourself, would refuse assistance from a brilliant researcher to help her with what I believe is the most difficult investigation of her life—to find her long-lost mother? Or to uncover why she has remained *long-lost* for thirty-plus years?"

"If I'm so good why would I need him?"

"Because he, unlike you, has no skin in the game. He can be dispassionate. Passion, while much desired in some activities, is an impairment in the expeditionary work of sleuthing. One who is engaged in the tedium of the investigative effort must be unemotional, untainted by sentiment, and able to see the facts when they are exposed.

"You, Theo, are not that removed from this case. I surmise that you are deeply troubled by what has landed on you in the past twenty-four hours. Who wouldn't be? I would offer my own services if my schedule were my own. It is not. Like you, I, too, have an emotional tie. A strong one. I was—am—anxious to find out if she is alive and if my brother's child survived. Finding her or what happened to her will bring closure. It would bring me peace, allow me to move on."

Theo's silence prompted another comment.

"Sometimes, Theo, life takes more from us than we are able to give. I lost my brother—all my family—all that was dear to me. Perhaps you, more than most, can understand how that feels. I'll leave you with this: The heart knows what the heart knows. No one can know more. Good luck to you, Theo. I wish only the best for you. May you find what you seek."

With that, he waited.

Theo said, "This student, does he understand what's at stake?"

"Yes. He is committed and discreet. More importantly, he is trustworthy. Added bonus: I'll pay all his expenses."

"I'm headed to San Francisco tomorrow. I'm booked on Southwest, Flight 935 at 6:45. That's *a.m.* Tell him if he wants to help, to be on it."

Ibrahim smiled. "Absolutely, my dear! He will be there."

"What's his name?"

"Kasim. Kasim Jabul."

"Oh, and professor . . . "

"Yes, my dear?"

"Tell him not to get in my way!"

7

San Francisco

It was an unusually bright sunny morning when Theo and Kasim exited the cab at 601 Vallejo St. in North Beach, Little Italy, one of the oldest areas of the city. They settled into a small table at the window and ordered espresso.

After a stiff introduction before boarding their flight in San Diego, they had kept talk to a minimum. Theo briefly outlined her plan, which was less of a plan and more of an immersion into the ambience of the locale. She had done all the public records research she could do online: mother's birthdate, marriage, father's death records, newspaper clippings of his heroism and his obituary. Now, she simply wanted to walk the streets, see the sights and feel whatever Zen stirrings might be conjured up when she trod in their footsteps. Perhaps it was closure she was seeking. It might have been Theo's way of mourning the two most significant people in her life. One, a decorated war hero who died before she was born; the other, a woman who was an enigma—the mother of whom she had no memory.

Kasim studied the barista at the bar, the bustle of customers, the busy waitress, and the street view outside the shop windows. "Do you think your mother worked here, at this coffee shop? And who, besides the current staff, do you think might remember her?"

Theo took in the vibe. Both the waitress and the barista were young, tattooed and sported multiple piercings. Neither could have been older than thirty. Suddenly feeling less sure of herself than she did when she boarded the plane that morning, her immersion plan hit her as being less strategy and more foolishness.

As early morning patrons winnowed down, the Goth-like waitress, crowned with an unnaturally deep black, spiky hairstyle, was looking less harried. Kasim motioned to her.

"Hiya, what can I get you?"

"Some information—Alaina," he said noting her nametag.

"So, is this where you pass me a hundred-dollar bill all folded up?"

Kasim laughed. "If I had a hundred you'd be first on the list!"

The waitress seemed charmed by the handsome young man. She looked interested. "You kinda look like Johnny Depp. You're not him, are you?"

Kasim smiled. "I don't know—I might be. Would that help jog your memory?"

Theo was impatient with the banter. She held up the photo of her parents standing in front of the café.

"This was taken in the late seventies. I know you're too young to know this woman, but I believed she worked here. Is there anyone here who might have been around then?"

"Sure. The owner, Sal. But he's not here. He'll be in later this afternoon, though. Around three."

Alaina studied the photo. "So, what'd she do? Rob a bank?"

Theo took the photo back. "Not that we know."

Outside the coffee shop, Theo held another photo of her mother in front of an apartment building. She scanned the street as if she thought something might look familiar.

"A few decades can make a big difference in a neighborhood, Theo. Are you planning to scour every street looking for that building?"

Theo stuffed the photo back in her bag and folded her arms, looking as deflated as she felt.

"I did the records search online before I left San Diego. I found her marriage to my father in 1975. Tracing her maiden name, I found her birth record, including the address of her mother—my other grandmother. I Googled the address, but that building was torn down in the early eighties. I guess I just hoped I might find where she and my father lived after their marriage. I guess . . . I hoped . . . it's an old neighborhood. I thought . . . maybe something would look familiar. This was a stupid idea."

"Look," he said. "We could come back here and talk to the owner this afternoon. That's a start. In the meantime, did you book a room yet? If not, there's a hotel a couple of blocks from here, on Columbus. We can walk there. We should get that settled before we do anything else."

"Sure. Makes sense."

The clerk at the Columbus Motor Inn looked doubtful. "We're booked. I only have one room with double beds. Will that work? I've got someone checking out tomorrow. You could have that one. In the meantime, this is all I have. It would only be for one night."

"It has two separate beds?" Theo asked.

"Yep. Both are queen size. It's on the third floor so it has a view of the wharf."

She looked at Kasim, who shrugged, looking amused. "It's okay with me, Theo."

They booked the room and headed for the elevator.

The room overlooked the corner of Columbus and Broadway.

Kasim checked the view. "Did he say a 'view of' the wharf? This is more looking 'in the direction of' the wharf. An important distinction."

Theo joined him. "If you crane your neck and lean out the window, maybe stand on the ledge, then, yeah, 'of' might almost be accurate."

"Do you have a preference?" she said, indicating the beds.

"I prefer the one closest to the window."

Theo nodded and set her duffel on the other. Kasim dropped his bag on the suitcase stand next to his and took out his laptop. He keyed in the hotel's Wi-Fi and started typing. "Theo, hand me those photos, the ones where they're standing in front of a building."

After a few minutes, Kasim's tapping on the keys stopped.

Theo, sitting cross-legged on the bed, looked up from the pile of printed documents spilling out of the open file on her lap. "Give up?"

"Theo, I think you should see this."

Theo peered over his shoulder. The screen showed the *San Francisco Examiner* headline dated Monday, February 26, 1979: "Congressman O'Keefe's Campaign Headquarters Ripped by Blast Sunday Morning—Two Dead!" Below it, the black and white photo of the building with most of its façade in rubble. Her eyes widened. The corner of the building that was not destroyed bore an Ionic column. It looked like the same column on the building in her mother's photo.

Kasim let it sink in. "This is where your mother worked, Theo. This is the building. May I see your photo—is there a date on it?"

"Nothing. But it had to be before February 1979. It's not damaged and she's dressed warmly. My guess is that it's just before. Maybe Ahmed took this photo to commemorate her getting the job. Ibrahim said she only worked there a few weeks before the bombing."

Kasim scribbled down the address from the newspaper. "We should go there. Today."

"What do you think we'll find?"

"I don't know. But we need to see what's around there."

"Kasim, that was nearly 35 years ago. Do you think it's still there? Wouldn't they have torn it down? What will that prove?"

"Just a gut feeling, Theo. Humor me."

They stood at the corner of the intersection of Chestnut and Mason Streets. The building that had once housed the campaign headquarters for Congressman Jack O'Keefe was situated on the corner and looked as it had in the photo. You wouldn't have guessed that decades ago a bomb had destroyed half of the ground-floor offices and taken two lives.

Theo gazed at the front of the building, which now had signage proclaiming mortgage loans at a 3.67 percent interest rate. She fished the photograph of her mother out of her purse and held it up.

"She was standing right there. Next to that column."

Kasim wasn't listening. He was doing a three-sixty, taking in all four corners of the intersection.

"Kasim?"

"Yeah, Theo, sorry. I was just trying to see how many of these buildings might have been here then.

"Theo, there!" he said, pointing to a three-story building mid-block.

Theo squinted at the sign, angled out from the building. "The sign says it's an art gallery."

"Yes. Now. But that might just be the ground floor," he said, heading at a fast clip. "It looks like apartments above."

Theo shrugged and picked up her pace to catch up.

The sign read, "Chestnut's Fine Art." The young man behind the counter greeted them, but before he could steer them to any of the pricey art pieces, Kasim asked about the apartments above the gallery.

"Oh, we don't have anything to do with those," he said. "If you're looking to rent, you should check with the manager on the first floor. They have their own entrance. It's around the corner. Off the alley. Up the stairs."

He directed them back out the door and to a private entrance at the side of the building. The plaque above the door read, "Atlanta Arms."

Kasim rang the bell. The old intercom crackled to life. "No vacancy," the man's gravelly voice shot out of the grid.

Kasim said. "We're just looking for information on someone who may have lived here in the late seventies."

"What?" came the voice.

"The late seventies. We're trying to locate a family member who may have lived here then."

There was a pause, then a buzzer, then the door bolt clicked open.

The door to apartment "101" with the "Manager" sign above it was cracked open, the security chain taut. A portion of a grizzled face peered out. "Who're you looking for?"

Theo took the lead. "I'm so sorry to bother you, sir. It's just that I was hoping to find out if my mother lived here once."

"Why don't you ask her?"

"She . . . ," Theo cleared her throat. Kasim spoke up. "She's passed away, sir. We're just . . . well, it probably seems strange, but we're just trying to put some closure to our loss."

The door banged shut. There was a clink as the chain slid back. The door reopened. The manager looked old enough to have been old in the seventies.

"What's yer names?" the old man said, tilting his head to look through his spectacles, which were perched on the end of his nose. He stared at Theo, then smiled. He motioned for them to follow him inside. "And speak up. I can't find my hearing aids."

The apartment must have been spacious, but it was difficult to tell with the clutter of what had to be decades of collecting, filling most of the usable space. The manager motioned for them to sit. Kasim moved several days, maybe weeks, worth of newspapers to make space for them on the couch.

Theo repeated their names—loudly.

"No need to shout," the old man said, fishing something out of his sweater pocket and inserting it into his right ear. He put another into the left ear and microphone feedback from the hearing aids screeched at them.

"I'm right here. Oh, that's better." He smiled.

He studied Theo for a moment. "You sure look like her."

"So I've been told."

He seemed to be sizing her up, scrutinizing her. "How old are you?"

"Thirty-six."

"You didn't stay with your mama."

It wasn't a question.

"My grandmother raised me."

He nodded. "That would make sense then. She was serious about something. I always thought she was on a mission. She had a roommate—a woman—and a boyfriend."

"You have an excellent memory," Kasim piped up. "That was a long time ago."

The old man leaned back in his chair and looked beyond them to the only window with the shade pulled up. He was quiet for a few moments, as if he were watching something play across and old memory.

"It was. A lot is pretty hazy. But some things just stick, you know. I remembered those girls. Your mother died in that explosion."

"You remember the explosion?"

"It was a damn big deal. Your mother and another person who worked there died."

"Do you remember any of Dena's friends, besides her roommate?" Kasim asked.

"Dena? Who's Dena?"

"Dena Hunter. That's who we're talking about," Theo added.

The old man smirked as if testing them. "Oh. So that was her name. It wasn't what I knew her by. Had a different name then. We all did."

Theo glanced at Kasim. "What name did she use . . . then?"

"Scarlett. Scarlett O'Hara." He laughed.

Theo gaped at him. "You're kidding."

"Nope. Most my tenants in those days didn't use their real names. Lotsa college students who were on sabbatical, if you know what I mean. Lotsa unrest then. Lotsa comings and goings. Sometimes I only rented a flat for a week at a time. They were all coming here from someplace else. They'd get their feet wet in this movement or that. Then, 'poof,' gone.

"It was like we all just woke up from dreamland, saw the world for what it was. It was way different than the sixties and early seventies. Not so much flower-power and groovy love stuff. That had pretty much petered out. Serious drugs and hardline pushers were out on the streets then. Got to be pretty dangerous. Of course, I didn't let any of those into my place. Kept it clean for the ones, like your mom, the serious types. She didn't do drugs. Pot maybe. But not the hard stuff.

"Like I said. She seemed to be on a mission. A lot of 'em were. Getting into the government and bringing change. That's what we were about. That was a couple years after the war—Vietnam. Whole different group of young people trying to fix things. Sit-ins and love-ins got momentary attention. But the real change had to come from inside the system. Grassroots movements. Poly-sci and law majors from Berkeley were all over the neighborhood in those days," he said, smiling. "You kids should look it up. Get a real history lesson."

"I'll bet it was exciting to be here then. Were you involved in some of those movements?"

He gave them a sideways grin. "I dabbled."

"So, you never knew her real name?"

The old man averted his eyes. "Naw. Didn't need to. Didn't want to. She looked like Scarlett O'Hara. That was enough for me. She was a real beauty."

Kasim said, "I take it you liked her?"

He nodded. "It was hard not to. Some of those kids were hard-pushers. Had a lot of anger. She was different. She was kind. Thoughtful. And had a sadness about her. I figured something really bad had happened to her. Like I said, she was on a mission of some sort. She never said. I never asked."

"How do you know she died in that explosion?"

"The cops. They came here after they found some records. They ID'd the dead girl."

"Who identified her?" Theo asked.

"Wasn't me. I heard they were real close to that bomb. What was left . . . well, there wasn't much left. I think the cops just did the math."

"I see," Theo said, looking away.

"I'm sorry to be the one to tell you."

"What about her roommate, the other girl?"

The old man shifted in his chair. "She never came back. I figured she got scared and took off."

Kasim spoke up. "I don't suppose you kept any of Dena's things? I realize it was a long time ago and all . . . just wondering if . . . "

"Yeah. I kept the stuff the cops didn't take."

He got up out of the chair with difficulty. "Look at this place. You really think I'd throw anything away?"

He headed into another room. Theo and Kasim heard scraping sounds as if boxes were being shoved about. He returned with a cardboard banker's box that had to be decades old and looked it.

"Here," he said, handing the box to Theo. "There's really not much in it. I only kept it because it reminded me of her. He looked at Kasim and nodded. "Seems like the right time for it to move on to family."

Theo thanked him and headed for the door, then stopped. "Her roommate," Theo said. "I don't suppose you remember her name?"

He smiled. "Melanie."

Theo nodded, "Of course."

In the hall, Theo turned. "Thank you, Mr. . . ."

The old man smiled and hit the buzzer to unlock the outer door.

"They called me Rhett. Rhett Butler."

"Rhett Butler" slid the chain back into place after the young couple left. He shuffled back into the dining room and toward the wall of boxes stacked on both sides. He didn't hear the knock on the door. The second round was louder.

"Bet they forgot to ask me something," he mumbled, heading back to the front door.

"Okay . . . okay . . . keep yer drawers on . . ." he said, sliding the chain back and pulling the door open.

"You!" he said, stunned. It had been over thirty years, but there was no mistaking who stood there.

"I thought I'd never see *you* again," he said, opening the door wider. "This must be the day for reminiscing. Come in."

8

They headed back down Columbus toward Vallejo and Caffé Trieste, hoping to catch the owner. The afternoon crowd was filling up the place. It took them thirty minutes before Sal Crivello joined them at the table.

"Yeah, I remember her," Sal said. "She worked here off and on during high school and college. She left for a few years, then came back after her husband was killed in Vietnam. She only worked a couple of weeks before she landed that job at the congressman's office. Guess you heard about that bombing. She was one of those who . . . ," his words trailed off, unfinished. He nodded to Theo. "Sorry for your loss. Damn shame."

Kasim spoke up, "I don't suppose you still have any employment records from back then?"

"Nope. That was a long time ago. My bookkeeper only keeps stuff three years. All those records have been long shredded. My wife might remember something, though. I'll check with her. She's in the back."

Sal headed back to the kitchen. A few minutes later, he returned with a woman in an apron.

"Hi, I'm Rosa," the amiable woman said, fanning herself and slipping into a chair. "Gets so hot back in that kitchen."

"Whatever you're baking smells scrumptious," Theo said.

"Biscotti. We can't keep them in stock!" Rosa said, laughing. "I have to make them four times a week and every day during the holidays."

"Honey," Sal said. "This is Dena's little girl. You remember Dena?"

Rosa smiled at Theo and patted her hand. "I sure do, honey. Your mama was a really nice kid. So sad what happened to her. I'm so sorry. Some people just have no luck."

Kasim spoke up. "We're just trying to piece together a little information about her. We were wondering if you remembered anything? Who she hung out with. If she dated anyone?"

Rosa turned to Theo, "She was very pretty, but with so much sorrow . . . " Rosa tilted her head and looked at Theo. "I see it in your eyes, too. You've lost someone—maybe too many."

Theo swallowed hard, banishing the thought of Frank that Rosa's comment suddenly evoked. Under other circumstances, it would have been easy to talk to this woman who seemed to have an uncanny sense about matters of the heart and about great loss. But that wasn't why she was there. Theo cleared her throat. "I never knew my mother. That's why we're trying to find out what we can about her life . . . and death."

Rosa nodded as if she understood. "I can tell you that she worked here during school years and then later, after her husband was killed. Was he your father?"

Theo nodded.

"I'm sorry, Theo. Life must seem so unfair."

Theo struggled to respond to that. Losing Frank had ripped open a big hole in her heart and shattered the hard shell around any feelings previously associated with the father and mother she never knew. That left her with emotional raw edges, vulnerable and, to her great embarrassment, unpredictable.

Theo's eyes watered up. She felt for a Kleenex and found a limp, mangled one in her jacket pocket. She blew her nose and dabbed beneath her eyes.

"Sinuses," she mumbled.

Rosa nodded. "Yeah. It's that time of year."

Kasim interjected: "So, then, you don't remember her talking about any friends? Maybe mentioning a few people she might have hung around with?"

Rosa shook her head. "Not really. Just about her little girl."

She turned to Theo, "She was so anxious to get enough money to bring you here, Theo. That's why she got that office job. Still, there was that sadness about her. She had a lot on her shoulders. First her husband, then her mother. So tragic. Some people are just born to struggle. The Sicilians have a saying, *Nun si po' aviri la carni senz' ossu.* It means 'you can't have meat without the bone.' It is true, in life you take the good with the bad."

Theo felt a twinge in her chest—another unwelcome reminder that thinking about her mother evoked more than simple curiosity.

Kasim interjected, "So, no one comes to mind? Anyone who might still be around that we could talk to?"

Rosa and Sal looked at each other and shrugged. "Only the young man she met later. He was nice. Oh, and her girlfriend. She was her roommate. We never saw any of them again after the . . . " she hesitated, "after the terrible bombing."

Rosa said, "I sure can't get over it! You really look like her, Theo . . . spitting image."

Theo managed a smile and a nod.

Theo and Kasim thanked the Crivellos for their time and rose to leave.

"Wait," Rosa said, disappearing into the back of the shop. A few moments later she reappeared with a pink bakery box, fragrant with the warm scent of anise. "These were just baked. Biscotti. Have some with your coffee later."

"We Sicilians think the day is much sweeter with biscotti in the morning!" Sal said, laughing.

"You come back to see us," Rosa added.

Theo's eyes watered up and she cleared her throat. "I—thank you," was all she could manage.

Kasim slipped his arm around her and they headed out toward Columbus and the hotel.

Kasim resumed his Internet search. He was buried in his computer and didn't hear Theo tell him she was going to step outside to get better cell phone reception. She could have switched to the hotel's Wi-Fi, but she didn't trust it to be as secure as her provider's 3G network.

Abby answered on the first ringtone. "Hey, Theo! About time you checked in with me. So, how's it going?"

"Better than I thought in some regards. We found the coffee shop where Dena worked until she got the job at the congressman's office. Then we located that building. You'd never guess there had been an explosion there. Then we found the actual apartment where she lived. Lots to tell you. The apartment manager remembered her and gave me a box of her effects that he had kept, along with about thirty-plus years' accumulation of other crap. The guy is a hoarder. Lucky for me!"

Abby cut in, "Great! Oh, and just who's the other factor in the 'we' equation?"

"Kasim. Kasim Jabul. He's a researcher for Ibrahim, who insisted he come with me. I resisted, but he's been pretty helpful. I'm not sure I would have found Dena's apartment building or the congressman's office without his help."

"Well, that's good to hear. Glad you're not going at this alone. So, what's in the box?"

"I haven't had a chance to look into it yet. I will as soon as we're done talking. I just wanted to check in with you."

"Appreciate that," Abby said. "So, how much longer do you plan to be there?"

"It depends on what I find in that box and what Kasim hacks into."

"Whoa! Hack? As in 'hacking'? Like, *WikiLeaks*? Didn't that guy go to jail?"

"No. Nothing like that. I used the term loosely. I just meant he's trying to see the kind of records he can find on the Internet—legally."

Abby processed what Theo told her against what she suspected Theo really meant. "I'm serious. Don't go hacking government stuff. People go to jail for that. You could wind up at Guantanamo."

Theo smirked. "Hacking could be profitable. Julian Assange won top prizes for journalism when he published sensitive leaked government security documents. My awards shelf is looking pretty sparse."

"Stop jerking me around!" Abby said, irritated. "Visiting you in federal prison isn't on my bucket list. Knock it off!"

"Calm down, Abs. Just messing with you!"

"Well, you certainly are in a much better frame of mind than when you left. So, is he cute?"

"Cute? What? Stop. It's not like that. He's just doing a job and, frankly, I'm grateful for the company." Theo shot back defensively.

"Oh, don't get your panties in a bunch. Just kidding. So, go find out what's in that box and call me back. I have the night off so I'm in my sweats, on the couch, watching old movies on the tube. Oh, it's raining ass-over-teakettles down here. How's the weather there?"

"We're clear. Not a cloud in the sky. I'll check back in after I dig into that box. Oh, and don't forget to feed my kitty."

"That monster's big enough to catch his own food! But don't worry. I'll see if I can rustle up a stray rat for his majesty!"

"He likes Fancy Feast Wild Salmon Florentine with Garden Greens."

"Privileged little prick!" Abby snorted.

"Thanks, Abs."

"You're welcome. You owe me. Big time!"

Theo's phone battery was just about dead when she clicked off. When she turned to head back to the room she was surprised by Kasim coming toward her. He looked agitated.

"Where were you?"

"I told you. I needed to make a call."

Kasim took a deep breath. "When I saw you were gone . . . I got worried."

"I'm right here. Actually, I was headed back to the room. So, any luck?"

"No. I've hit nothing but stone walls. I'll keep trying, though."

Back in the room, Theo settled onto her bed with the box "Rhett" had given her. Kasim pulled up a chair.

Rhett had been right. There wasn't much. Theo wondered what the police had taken. She pulled out a heavy Navy pea coat, a couple sweaters, wool bell-bottom slacks, suede boots that laced up to the knee—very fashionable in the seventies—and a couple of miniskirts. Under the clothes were a hairbrush, eye shadow, and a lipstick that had long lost its pearly sheen. The only underwear was a silk flesh-toned slip. No papers. Nothing more.

"That's it?" Kasim looked at her.

"You see it. There's nothing else. Just her clothes. Not even all her clothes, I'll bet. There's no jewelry. There's not even more underwear. Why would the cops take her underwear? DNA testing?"

Kasim did a quick Internet search and found several sites. They all listed the first DNA forensics testing for biological material and bodily fluids wasn't begun until 1985.

"I don't think the cops are the ones who took her personal items," Kasim said.

"You think it was someone else?"

"Rhett was enamored enough to keep her stuff. Wouldn't surprise me a bit if he kept some very personal items for himself," Kasim said. "I'll bet he was holding out on us."

"That's just creepy," Theo said and scowled.

"You think we should confront him?"

"I think if he kept her underwear, he may have kept other things. Documents. Anything else about her that he needed to feed his weirdo fetishes."

"Before we head back over there, Theo, check the pockets of the coat."

Theo dug through the pockets and came up with nothing. "There's nothing here to give us any clues about her—except that she dressed like a hippie," Theo said.

9

An ambulance and several squad cars were parked on both sides of Chestnut Street when they got there. As they walked toward the side alley, the young man they had spoken to earlier at the gallery saw them.

"There," he said to the uniformed officers taking his statement. He pointed to Theo and Kasim. "That's them."

A detective in street clothes with a badge hanging from a lanyard around his neck motioned to them.

"A word with you," he said directing them to the opposite side of the street. "I'm Detective Gault, this here's my sidekick Detective Stern. And whom do we have the pleasure?"

"I'm Kasim Jabul. This is Theo Hunter."

"Well, Mr. Jabul and Miss Hunter, I understand that you were asking about these apartments earlier today. Did you happen to talk to the manager, Mr. Slagg?"

"We spoke to the man in apartment 101," Theo offered. "But he didn't tell us his name."

The detective looked from her to Kasim. "Uh huh. So, what did he tell you?"

"We were . . ." Theo started, but Kasim jumped in.

"We wanted to see if there were any vacancies."

"I see," said Gault. "So, the sign in the window," he said, turning and indicating the bay window with a No Vacancy sign clearly displayed, "wasn't a clue?"

"I don't recall seeing that. We were on that side of the street. Couldn't see the window at that angle," Kasim said.

Gault nodded. "So, did you?"

"Did we . . . what?" Kasim asked.

Detective Stern spoke up. "Did you talk to Slagg?"

"Yes. We talked to him. Like I said, detective."

"Inside?"

"Inside? You mean *inside* his apartment?"

"Yes," Kasim said. "So, what's this about?"

"Mr. Slagg is . . . deceased," Stern added. "Apparently, he tripped on something. Hit his head. Accident. Leastwise that's what it looks like now."

Kasim looked at Theo. She spoke up. "But we just talked to him. He seemed fine. Not dizzy or uncoordinated. What happened?"

"See," Gault said. "That's just what we were about to ask you? So, where do you live now that you're interested in one of these apartments?"

"We're at the Columbus Motor Inn. We're just here a couple of days," Theo said

"Listen," Gault was talking. "I'm sure you can imagine we might have a couple of questions. I don't suppose you two could come down to our office and give us a statement? Wouldn't take long. It's just that our team can't wrap up until we say so. We need to get the body to the medical examiner and all."

Theo shot a sideways glance at Kasim. He nodded.

"Sure, we can go with you."

Gault and Stern ushered them into an office at the police headquarters on Third Street and offered coffee, which they declined.

"So. You two looking to move to San Francisco?"

Kasim took the lead. "We're in San Diego right now. I'm a research assistant at San Diego State and Theo's a reporter for a local newspaper. We both love San Francisco and thought, 'We're young, why not.'" He looked at Theo and smiled. She took the cue.

"I've always thought it would be fun and exciting to cover the beat on the street here."

Gault nodded and glanced at Stern. "Usually, you get the job first before moving. Aren't you two doing it ass-backwards?"

"Maybe," Kasim said, grabbing Theo's hand and kissing the back of it. "Makes it kinda romantic, don't you think?"

Theo smiled demurely and shrugged. "Definitely!"

A uniformed officer knocked at the door and opened it. "Detectives, may I see you a moment."

Gault and Stern excused themselves. Theo turned to Kasim and started to speak when he pulled her close and kissed her. She started to pull back when he rolled his eyes toward the ceiling and the camera mounted so that it pointed right at them. She saw it and pulled away, giggling. "Stop! What if they come back in?"

"Honey," Kasim said, just loud enough for any microphone to pick up. "Why don't we go to Pier 39 for dinner tonight? Doesn't chowder sound really good?"

"Oh, and fried calamari. I've got a real craving for that! Maybe even some raw oysters on the half-shell!" She added, giggling again.

"Why do you say things that just make me want to kiss you!" He said, pulling her close and nibbling her ear. "Keep it up," he whispered.

Theo suddenly pulled back. "Honey, what if we can't get jobs here right away?"

Kasim laid his finger on her lips. "I told you. I can practically transfer to San Fran State. My profs will give me glowing reviews. We can make it on my salary alone for a few months. So, don't you worry . . . " He didn't get to finish.

Gault swept back in the door and announced that they didn't have any further questions, but added, "Just leave your San Diego addresses with the clerk outside. In case we have any further questions."

Before they left the building, Kasim pulled out his cell phone and told Theo to pose with the intake clerk, which she did. He snapped several photos.

Outside, Theo said, "You think they suspected us? I thought they said it was an accident. He tripped and fell."

"They acted like it might be more. Right now, I think we're their prime suspects if the medical examiner says it was anything other than an old man's tragic trip and fall."

"What was all that posing and picture-taking about?"

He pulled out his phone and showed her a close-up of the policeman's ID.

"What are you planning to do?"

"Get into the cold case evidence room," he said, motioning her toward the Grey Line bus that pulled into the stop.

"Are you nuts?"

"We need to see what they have on your mom, Theo. We're going to have to pick up the pace."

They got off at Ghirardelli Square. Kasim pulled out his phone again. Within minutes a Prius with an "Uber" decal pulled to the curb. They got in. "Change of plans," Kasim said. "Can you take us to San Francisco State?"

"No problem," the driver said, easing away from the curb and into traffic.

10

They disappeared into the university's administration building, caught an elevator to the personnel office where Kasim asked for various employment forms. He stuffed them into his backpack. Then, he summoned another Uber and they returned to the hotel.

"I know you're going to tell me what that was all about," Theo said when they were back in their room.

"We need to look like a couple in love with the city and wanting to move here."

"You think they're following us?"

"I'd be surprised if they weren't."

He pulled his laptop from the backpack and opened up a new program. Within minutes he had the policeman's ID up on the screen and was manipulating the officer's photo, replacing it with his. Theo watched—horrified.

"You can't be serious! You can't just waltz back into the police station and get into the evidence room!"

He looked up at her with genuine surprise. "Why not?"

"Because that's Hollywood stuff—not real life."

"Do you think Hollywood just makes it up? As with everything in fiction and movies, there's a basis in truth. This has been done, Theo. It's proven."

"You're gonna get caught."

"Me? You mean us, don't you?"

He turned the computer around to show her two perfect IDs. One for him. One for her.

"Okay, wiseass. And just how are you going to get those printed up—good enough to look real? Besides, we don't have cops badges."

Kasim ignored her. He picked up his cell and punched in a number. Theo heard a voice on the other end and Kasim said, "Sending."

"So," he said, turning off the computer. "Where do you want to eat?"

They walked to Pier 39 and got a table at Fog Harbor Fish House near the window. The New England-style chowder was served up in a sourdough bread bowl. It was hot, creamy-thick, and delicious. Theo ordered her fried calamari and that disappeared faster than the soup.

Out on the pier they watched tourists tossing scraps to the barking sea lions.

Kasim wrapped his arms around her and pulled her in for a long kiss.

Theo sensed there was more than acting on Kasim's part. She pulled back from his embrace and said through a smile, "Was this to impress our tail?"

"No. We lost them after the university. This was for me."

He leaned in again. Theo stopped him. "No, Kasim. I've got—"

Kasim looked into her eyes. "I know. Frank. And he's MIA right now. So that makes this all the more difficult."

"What?"

"What I'm about to say."

"Don't!" Theo said. "Don't say he's not coming back. Right now, hope is all I have. I'm not even sure I really believe in that. So, don't make it any more difficult."

"I'm not asking you to, Theo. I'm just letting you know how I feel. That's all."

He took her arm and they walked back to Embarcadero and hailed a cab. Kasim gave the driver an Oakland address.

They pulled up to an industrial warehousing district. Kasim paid the driver and they headed toward an office. There was a light on. Kasim hit the buzzer and the door latch clicked. Theo stopped him.

"Last time we did this an old man died."

"It's okay. You have to trust me."

"I don't have to trust anybody."

"That's right, Theo. But you can trust me."

Inside, Kasim typed numbers into a keypad on another door. There was a click followed by an electronic whine as a camera over the door scanned them both. Moments later, a mail flap in the door opened as a manila envelope with a noticeable bulge was pushed through. That was it.

Kasim and Theo exited and walked a short distance to the main street. Kasim used his cell phone to call a cab.

Within fifteen minutes, they were at 1245 Third Street, San Francisco's main police headquarters. He produced two large plastic sleeves attached to lanyards. Kasim handed one to Theo.

She stared at the official looking SFPD ID with her photo. Beside it was a silver seven-pointed star, a very authentic looking police officer's badge. Her eyes widened. "How did you . . ."

"Elementary. I know a guy who knows a guy," he said, slipping the lanyard around his neck. "For the price, they'd better do the trick."

Theo did the same with hers. "I don't have a good feeling about this."

"The evidence vault is in the basement," Kasim said. "We should have no problem getting in. We're thirty minutes into the shift change."

Theo said, "And that's critical because?"

"We've got hours before the next shift comes on duty. We want to be done and out of here long before that. The outgoing shift has to call in anyone in the vault and have them re-sign the register log with the new shift. We don't want that. No telling what the new guy will want. Besides, thirty minutes should be enough time."

"Done this before, have you?"

Kasim ignored her.

"Old evidence boxes are stored in the back. Not likely we'll run into anybody else in that section. Now, let's get a move on."

They had no trouble getting to the basement. At the desk, they signed in with their fake names and badge numbers and were given the location of the old cold-case files.

The files were chronological, which helped, but it still took nearly fifteen minutes to locate the five evidence boxes relating to the bombing incident in 1979. A separate box was devoted to each of the two people identified as having been killed. Theo stopped at the box marked "Dena Hartsohn."

"Kasim, here it is."

He pulled it down and they stared at the plastic pouches that held the remnants of clothing with dark crusted stains that could only be blood. The box also held Dena's personal effects that the police gathered at her apartment. A blouse and pair of slacks. A purse with a wallet. A rent receipt for the apartment on Chestnut Street. The Payee's name was ripped off. There was a wallet with ID for Dena Hartsohn with only a few dollars. That was it.

"Hartsohn," Theo whispered to Kasim. "That's her maiden name. She didn't use her married name."

"I'm thinking that's significant," he said

"Yeah. Interesting. Like someone who didn't want to be traced."

"Or didn't want anyone connecting her to her husband and his family—you, to be specific."

Kasim had gone through the other four boxes in the time it took Theo to look at and touch what had been her mother's items from her last moments. Theo took out her phone and snapped photos of all the items, including the clothing tags.

"We're done here," he said. "Time to get going."

They checked out and were making their way to the elevator when they saw Detective Stern waiting. He was pushing the call button and didn't look up. He didn't see them. Kasim saw the stairwell door and pushed Theo through it.

"Go! Quick!" he whispered.

They just made it to the next level up when they heard the door below them open. Kasim and Theo pressed against the wall, just out of sight of the man peering up.

Hearing nothing, Stern headed back to the elevator just as the doors opened. A young female officer greeted him.

"Detective Stern . . . to what do we owe the pleasure?"

While Stern and the officer chatted, Theo and Kasim made their way to the main lobby and out the door. Their luck held. A cab was waiting at the curb.

11

Theo didn't breathe until they were back at the hotel and in their room. She sat on the bed, he on the chair. They just stared at each other. Then, they broke into laughter.

"I can't believe we pulled that off!" she said through hysterics.

Kasim shook his head. "Me neither."

Theo stopped laughing. "What do you mean? I thought you were old hat at this cloak-and-dagger stuff. At least that's how it sounded."

"Well, I do have some connections. But honestly, Theo, I've really only seen it done in movies."

"What? What if they had been suspicious of us?"

"How? Fake names. Fake badge numbers."

"They have our pictures."

"Well, that whole facial recognition is really not as accurate as they'd have you believe. On TV, in the movies, yeah. Helps to move the plot along. But in reality, not so much. Besides, I'm not in any databases."

"Well, I just might be!" she shot back.

"Still, I don't think you have anything to worry about. They're not going to connect the two phony cops with the sweet young couple looking to move to San Fran. Won't happen. TV stuff. Honest. I don't know about you, but I could use a drink," he said, pulling out a flask.

"Vodka. I'll get some ice. Need a mixer? There's a soda dispenser where the ice machine is located down the hall."

"Yeah. 7-Up or Sprite."

He disappeared out the door and returned shortly. He mixed her drink and took his straight with ice.

He downed his and poured another. Theo sipped hers as she studied the photos she'd taken of the evidence box contents. Disappointed that they hadn't been more help in her search, she gulped down her drink and fixed another.

"You know what bothers me," she began. "Her ID had her maiden name, not her married name. She must have filled out an employment form. Why didn't she list my grandmother as next of kin? Why didn't she mention a child?"

Kasim studied the photo of the ID. "She probably never listed an address in San Diego, only the apartment on Chestnut. That's why."

"But *why*?" Theo blurted.

Kasim looked up. "I know this is hard, Theo. But your mother was on some sort of mission. I don't think she wanted anyone to know how to contact her family."

"You think she was responsible for that bombing, don't you?"

Kasim shook his head. "I don't know. Right now, we just have scraps of information and not much else."

He went back to his computer. Theo continued to scroll through the photos on her phone.

"Kasim!"

"What?"

"Look at the clothes in the box old Rhett Butler gave us. Then look at the size on the label of the clothes from the evidence box."

He stared. Then shrugged. "What am I looking for?"

"The size," she said triumphantly. "They're not the same size. Rhett's box has size six. These," she pointed to the photos, "are size ten. A size ten doesn't wear a size six and vice-versa! The evidence box doesn't contain my mother's clothes. The police must have collected the wrong items from the apartment. These must have been the other girl's things."

Kasim was nodding. "That sneaky bastard. Old Rhett gave them the wrong stuff!"

"Yeah. That old guy was in love with her. He probably gave the wrong items to the police on purpose. But why? Do you think he figured she escaped? Do you think he thought she was alive?"

Kasim thought for a moment. "I think he *knew* she was. I think he was protecting her."

"And now he's dead. We'll never know the truth."

"Unless . . . there's more stuff still there in his apartment."

Theo set her empty glass down with a thud. "You can't be serious! I've had enough breaking and entering for one night. Besides, the whole place is locked up tight."

"I'm not without skills, Theo. I think I can get us in."

She started to say his plan was crazy. But crazy seemed to be the ruling factor for everything they'd done so far.

"Besides, how hard could it be to get into the apartment?" Kasim said. "We've already done the unthinkable and got away with it."

It was nearly midnight when they headed out the door, bound for the Atlanta Arms on Chestnut Street.

They expected a police guard to be posted on the door. There wasn't one, but the door was bolted from within and required a key. Just then, they heard footsteps. Someone was coming down the walkway and headed up the stairs.

Kasim wrapped his arms around Theo and pressed his face close to hers just as a young woman approached. She was balancing her cellphone on her shoulder and lugging grocery bags. Kasim made eye contact.

"Let me help you with those bags."

Still engaged on her phone, she nodded and handed them to him. She slid her key into the lock. Kasim pushed the door open and gave her back her bags.

She mouthed a silent "thank you," and hurried down the hall toward her own unit, her phone still pressed to her ear.

Kasim caught the door before it slammed shut.

"That was luck," Theo whispered.

Inside, they headed toward the manager's apartment. Yellow crime-scene tape was still "X'd" across the door. Kasim fiddled with the lock, mastered it, and they slipped inside. He threw the deadbolt for insurance.

Kasim motioned to Theo to keep the flashlight beam low so it wouldn't shine up on the windows and be seen from outside. The light beam slid over the worn carpet and old couch where Theo and Kasim had sat earlier. She moved it back toward the old man's club chair. There was no indication that this area was where Mr. Slagg, alias Rhett Butler, had fallen. They slipped past the seating area, heading toward the doorway where, earlier that day, Slagg had disappeared and returned bearing Dena's banker's box. They both stopped immediately when the dark stain on the carpet glimmered as the light slid across it. It was still wet.

"That must be where he . . . " Theo didn't finish.

Kasim nodded. "Yeah."

She moved the light toward the boxes stacked five to six feet up the wall—all the walls—a crumbling banker's box bas-relief. More boxes filled the floors, were piled atop the dining room table, under the table, and stacked on the built-in dining room hutch. It looked like a miniature warehouse for hoarders.

"Look at this stuff," Theo said. "How could he live like this?"

"Classic compulsive hoarder." Kasim added. "Textbook!"

As she trained the light over the boxes, they could see that each box was clearly labeled by year. They started to sift through the decade's worth of stacked boxes until they found the 1970s. From the scrape marks on the dusty floor, they followed what had been Slagg's earlier trail to a box labeled "1979."

"This has recently been pulled out," Kasim said, indicating the marks in the dust. There was a short hallway that connected the dining room to the bedroom.

"There's no windows in the hallway, we can turn on the overhead light and get a better look."

The hallway had its own clutter. Bundled newspaper and magazine stacks lined the whole of one wall, leaving only a marginal path. He hauled the box into the hall, found the wall switch, then shut the door. He flipped the switch and a weak bulb in a wall sconce sputtered awake as the patter of nocturnal activity rustled around them.

"Roaches," Theo shuddered. "I hate roaches!"

"They're more afraid of us that we are of them," Kasim offered, pulling off the lid. The box contained what they expected, more women's clothes. Theo checked the labels. "Size six! This is more of Dena's stuff!"

Voices in the outer hallway startled them. Someone fiddled with the mailbox by the front door, slammed it shut and headed up the stairs, giggling in concert with a companion. They waited until they heard a door close.

"We should take this and get out of here," Kasim said.

When they were sure no one else was in the outer hallway, they slipped outside and secured the door. They made their way back to the hotel.

Theo pulled off her jacket. "Listen, I'm not touching another thing until I've taken a shower. I feel itchy. Contaminated."

Kasim was on his computer when she emerged from the steamy bathroom, in sweats and her damp hair pulled back in a ponytail.

"Better?" he said, glancing up from the screen.

"I've felt cleaner after dumpster diving! How could anyone live like that?"

Kasim smirked. "Listen, when I was thinking about going into social service work, I volunteered to do health checks on seniors living in some of the flophouses down around Island and Fifteenth. You think old Rhett's place was something, you haven't seen the half of it."

"Is that what made you switch majors?"

"I figured I'd get burned out pretty quick. It's tough, Theo. Seeing how people's lives have disintegrated like that." He shook his head. "I just don't have the temperament for that work.

"Then, I thought I might like archaeology. You ever been on a dig?"

Theo shook her head "no."

"Ha! Talk about creepy-crawlies! You haven't lived until you've dived into a deep hole or clawed your way into a cave. Lots of surprises there."

She gave him an eyebrow raise and a shudder. "Thanks. That's another pleasant image I'll have to grapple with in my sleep tonight!"

Kasim turned his attention to the banker's box. "Okay, let's see what surprises this little treasure holds."

They pulled out more clothing—size six—and more personal items that belonged to Dena. A hairbrush. Some cosmetics. A macramé purse. A framed photograph of Dena and Jim. The photo was identical to the black and white photo Theo found in her grandmother's garage. There was also a manila envelope with a round coffee-cup stain and dog-eared edges. Inside was a letter.

Sweetheart, I can't say much about where I'm headed. This war is over. I have one last mission, then I'll be home to you. I think about you every day and try to picture your tummy getting bigger.

I'm glad the morning sickness has ended. I only wish I could be there to hold you. I miss you so much. I'm relieved knowing that you're staying with mom. She'll take good care of you. When I get back, we can rent one of the cottages if there's a vacancy—or find another place. It will be like our honeymoon—all over again. I promise!

Take care of yourself. Eat right. I'll be home before you know it. I love you, honey, and miss you more every day.

Jim

12

Theo sat on the edge of the bed staring at the letter in her hand. The masculine scrawl that had been her father's handwriting blurred and swam before her. She glanced up at Kasim just as her eyes brimmed over. He spanned the distance between them and pulled her into his arms. She cried. Big painful sobs. She cried for the loss of the father she never knew. She cried for her mother's loss. She cried for her own loss of both parents. And when she thought she couldn't cry any more, she cried for Frank.

Kasim said nothing. He simply held her against his chest and rocked back and forth, comforting her as parent might a child coming to grips with an unexplainable heartbreak. If he was offering more than a caring shoulder to cry on, it wasn't obvious. He never made the moves that would have crossed that line.

When the sobbing stopped, Theo pulled back, wiping her tears with the back of her hand, embarrassed. "I'm sorry," she said.

Kasim disappeared into the bathroom and emerged with a damp face towel. "Here, this will feel good and take down some of that heat."

"Am I red?"

"Let's just say you look like someone who's been crying."

Theo nodded and did as instructed. The cool, damp cloth did help, especially with the sudden headache that had erupted with the sobbing. She wiped her face and handed it back to him. "Thanks."

"No problem. Need another?"

She shook her head. "No, that won't happen again."

"I'm no expert, but it seems like it should've happened a long time ago."

"I keep my feelings in check. Life has always been easier that way."

"Nothing's easy when it comes to life, Theo. I do know something about the results of pressure buildup. Bottling up anything usually leads to consequences. I'm glad you had this little meltdown. You needed it."

Theo headed to the bathroom. When she returned, she was composed and determined. She folded the letter and slipped it back into the envelope.

"I can't believe old 'Rhett' told us he didn't know her real name. You know he must've gone through everything in this box. I wonder what other little surprises that creep hung onto all these years."

Theo weeded through the clothing. Nothing. Her mother's purse was all that remained. It was a macramé satchel, common to the era, with a zipper closure and a blue, glass-beaded tassel. Theo wondered if it might be homemade and if her mother was the crafter. Inside she found a small wallet with an ID card, the kind that wallets come with. The name listed was "Dena Hartsohn." The address was the San Francisco apartment that was listed on Dena's mother's death certificate. Nothing else except four single dollar bills. Someone had scribbled numbers in the border of one of them in red ink: 549.979.1522. Theo figured it might be a phone number.

"That's it. That's all there is," she said, deflated. "There's nothing here. Big dead-end."

Theo repacked the box with Dena's things and set it in a corner by the window.

"I guess that's it. We might as well return to San Diego tomorrow. The trails just disappear into the past. Here, we're no closer to finding out what happened to her than we were in San Diego."

Kasim had been studying something on his computer. He looked up. "I think there's one more thing we should check out.

"What would that be?"

"The retired congressman. What if he has records somewhere? What if he remembers her? What if he can shed some light on what happened?"

"That's a lot of what-if's. Doubtful."

He shrugged. "What else do we have? Don't give up so easily. We found where she lived. We have her personal effects. These were unthinkable milestones before we got here. We're on the right track, Theo. This is not the time to toss in the towel."

"You don't even know if O'Keefe is still in San Francisco? He might be dead."

Kasim turned his computer around. "He's in the Azure Hills Assisted Living Home in Corte Madera. It's about a thirty-minute drive north, up the 101 Highway.

"Tomorrow morning, we'll take a little drive."

Theo walked over to the window. "What's that going to prove?"

"I'm not sure, Theo. He might have some recollection that will be a clue. Anything at this point will lead us somewhere else."

"We've found lots of clues—all dead ends. I'm done. I just want to go home and forget about all this."

Theo crossed the room and grabbed her jacket. "I need some fresh air."

Kasim closed his computer. "Okay. I'll get my jacket."

"Alone. I just need to be—alone."

"It's nearly 1 a.m. Are you nuts?"

"Fine. Come with me but just be a shadow. That means keep your mouth shut."

They headed down Columbus Avenue, crossed over to Leavenworth Street, and followed that to Fisherman's Wharf. A smattering of tourists still occupied a few of the open-air tables outside a bar.

Theo headed toward the furthest corner of the wharf with the view of the bay and the Golden Gate Bridge in the distance. Kasim followed. They stood at the wooden railing. Below, small fishing boats moored there, bobbed. The water lapping against their hulls and the distant warning knell of the buoys were the only sounds. Even the sea lions were silent. Fog was settling in around the towers of the bridge that spanned the bay and the strait that connected with the Pacific Ocean.

"You could fall in love with this city," Theo said.

Not hearing anything from Kasim, she turned to look at him.

"Oh, am I permitted to speak? I wasn't sure if that was an invitation, or simply a rhetorical statement."

"Don't be an ass," she said.

He leaned against the railing.

"You know that bridge has been featured in nearly 75 movies, 32 TV shows, 30-plus video games, and 13 songs—that we know of," he added.

Theo glared at him. "You're a walking encyclopedia. Do you actively practice storing-up useless trivia for a particular reason—or is it that you just can't help yourself?"

Kasim smiled. "Both, I guess. Facts and figures, it's what I do. It's a mood killer that's for sure," he added. "Not the best pick-up line, either."

Theo smiled. Finally.

"I have a photo of them with the bridge looming above. They were in love. You could see it. Then everything just fell apart."

"He died, Theo. That's a game changer for anyone."

"How could she? How could she take up with a man who railed against everything her husband died for?"

Kasim looked out at the bay. "It probably wasn't like that. She was lonely. Maybe he was, too. They fell in love. Love is blind, you've heard that, right?"

"It's no use. I can't rationalize her behavior. I just don't get it. I won't ever be able to forgive her."

"Never say 'never,' Theo. Never is a very long time."

She shivered. "Okay, enough of the pep talk. Let's go back."

They headed back, unaware of the figure lurking, watching them from the shadows.

13

Azure Hills Assisted Living was a sprawling California Mission-style complex nestled at the foot of the Ring Mountains, overlooking San Francisco Bay. Theo and Kasim parked the rental car in the "visitor" spot and headed into the main building. Kasim had gotten prior authorization from an administrator earlier that morning under the pretext of an article he was writing for the U.S. House of Representatives on retired legislators.

"Right this way," the perky assistant said, guiding them down the hall to the dayroom where the white-haired elder statesman sat in a wheelchair, facing the large bay window that overlooked a grassy expanse. A man-made pond sputtered a plume of water at its center.

"Congressman," she said gently, "Congressman, you have visitors."

Congressman Jack O'Keefe gazed up at Kasim and Theo and smiled. "You'll have to excuse me if I don't get up," he said offering them his hand.

Kasim made the introductions and they settled into the chairs.

"It was good of you to see us on such short notice, sir," Kasim said. "We're only here one more day before we head back to San Diego."

"Well, it just so happens that my appointment calendar had an opening," O'Keefe said and smiled.

"Congressman," Theo started but was interrupted.

"You look vaguely familiar, young woman. Do we know each other?"

"No, sir. I get that a lot. I must have one of those faces," she said, clearing her throat. "We have a long list of your accomplishments during your time in the House, sir, but we really need just a little something that gives a more personal perspective."

O'Keefe nodded.

Kasim broke in, "Congressman, you were one of the principal crafters of the Palestinian Peace Accords during your tenure on the Hill. With all the good that was done in that regard, not everyone felt that we did all we could to stem the violence that resulted from that agreement."

"You're talking about the Mideast?"

"Specifically, I'm referring to the bombing of your campaign headquarters."

"Oh," the old man said, slumping back in his chair.

"That must have been a horrendous time for you. Two of your staff members died in the explosion. The perpetrators were never caught. Is that right, sir?

"That's right! The bastards got away with it!" he said, raising his hand in a gesture of disgust. His bottom lip trembled and he stopped talking. He just stared out the window.

Theo shot Kasim a nod. "Congressman," he continued, "were there any records that might have pointed the finger to the bomber? Could it have been someone you knew?"

The old man sat up straighter and looked directly at Kasim. "The PLO! Those bastards! They had a cell in San Francisco. Picked my office because of my work to bring peace. They didn't want peace! They wanted bloodshed!"

His voice carried beyond their discussion. An older couple playing cards at a table across the room glanced in their direction.

"Congressman," Theo cut in, "we didn't mean to upset you. It's just that it would help so much if we could . . ."

The old man turned and stared, registering confusion. Then he spoke. "That's it! It's *you*! You're her! But . . . she died! Are you here to blame me?"

Theo leaned in. "No, sir. I . . ."

"You're her—that young woman—"

He put his hands to his face to cover his eyes and started to sob. "You're dead! They killed you! They wanted me . . . but they killed . . . *you!*"

Theo looked up just as a woman and two orderlies were headed in their direction.

Theo placed her hand on Congressman O'Keefe's knee. "I'm so sorry. We didn't mean to upset you."

The officious-looking woman shot Theo an almost smile. "I think that will be all."

The orderly pulled the old man's wheelchair away and headed back down the hall. Congressman Jack O'Keefe was still sobbing.

"What did you think you were doing?" the administrator hissed.

"We only asked him about . . ." Theo didn't get to finish.

The administrator turned to the other orderly. "See that our guests are escorted out—and off the property." With that, she turned on her heel and headed in the direction the congressman had been taken.

"Well, that went well," Theo said as Kasim merged back onto the highway.

"Actually," Kasim said, "It did. At least we know that everyone believed your mother died in the explosion. Apparently, no one suspected her of being involved."

Theo stared out the window as the car sped down 101 back toward the Golden Gate Bridge and the city.

"We don't know that's true, do we? What we know is that a senile old man didn't suspect her. That doesn't make it so."

They were heading through the lobby when the clerk called to them. "Are you still interested in that other room?"

Theo looked at Kasim. "Is there any reason to stay here any longer? It just seems that we've hit a brick wall."

"Theo, I'd like to try one more possibility. Are you willing to give it one more day?"

"Okay. One day. Then, we're done here."

"Oh, and Theo, I don't think we need another room. Unless you do."

Theo thanked the clerk and told him they would stay with just the one room for one more night.

"Okay. So? What's this last-ditch effort you have up your sleeve?"

Kasim suggested they order in pizza while he continued work on the computer. Theo didn't ask what he was up to. She didn't want to know. She just hoped it didn't include hacking into a government website.

They attacked the pepperoni and cheese pizza with gusto and polished off a bottle of Chianti while Kasim concentrated on whatever it was he was doing on the computer. Theo made a list of the items in her mother's box they'd excavated from Mr. Slagg's (aka Rhett Butler's) apartment. She was transferring her mother's belongings into a plastic bag for travel the next day. When she lifted the macramé purse, she heard a crackle—as if there were paper inside. "Huh? What's that?"

Kasim glanced up from the computer. "Did you say something?"

"Sounds like there's some paper in the purse."

Theo slipped her hand around inside the purse. It was empty, yet she heard the crackle sound again. "Maybe something's stuck in the lining."

She felt along the lining and discovered uneven stitching along the seam. "Looks as though it was ripped, then resewn," she mumbled. She fiddled with it, trying to work a thread loose. When that failed, she got her tweezers and plucked at the stitching until one of the stitches broke. She pulled the thread out until she had a three-inch opening, just wide enough to slip two fingers in.

"Huh, it *is* paper."

Gripping it between her fore- and middle fingers, Theo worked it out through the slit. With care, she pulled out a multi-folded paper. Decades of storage at the bottom of the box had flattened it until its folds were imprinted with age and ink residue. Gingerly, she unfolded it.

On it, a crudely-drawn diagram was sketched in ink. There were four free-hand rectangles. Each was labeled sequentially: Toilet, Fred, Jack and Break Room. The area that abutted "Jack's" square contained a large "X." At the bottom of the page was the notation: Work Area/ Reception/ & Dena, then a series of numbers that could have been a phone number.

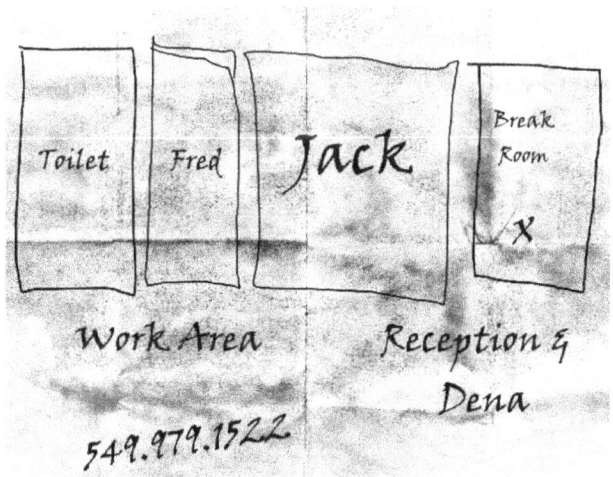

The numbers seemed familiar. Theo pulled her mother's wallet from the purse and found the dollar bill with the numbers. They were identical.

"Kasim!"

He glanced up, startled. "Jeezus! Theo, you scared the crap outta me! What's wrong?"

"Look!" She handed him the limp paper and the dollar bill.

He studied them. "Shit!" He looked at Theo, who looked as if she'd gone three shades paler. "You know what this is?"

She nodded.

"It's a schematic of the ground floor of that building."

Kasim pulled up the article about the explosion and read out loud: "At 9:45 a.m. on Sunday, February 25, 1979, the campaign offices of Congressman Jack O'Keefe were rocked by an explosion. The congressman was not in his office at the time; however, two of his staff were. They have been identified as: chief of staff Fred Walter and office assistant Dena Hartsohn. Both staff members were killed . . . " He stopped reading.

Kasim said, "The 'X' marks where the bomb was placed in the break room, next to Jack O'Keefe's office. The numbers on the paper are the date and time the detonator was set to explode."

"And the numbers on the dollar bill are the same," Theo said. "It was a code for date and time of the explosion."

Kasim said, "Theo—"

"Yeah. I know," she said. Her eyes riveted on his. "It's the smoking gun. Dena knew."

14

Theo sat on the edge of the bed. The paper with the schematic of Congressman Jack O'Keefe's office lay beside her. Her thoughts were tumbling over themselves with excuses. Explanations. Rationalizations. Anything. Any possibility that could refute the damning evidence she found in Dena's purse. But there were none. What the paper said to her was clear. It couldn't be more so.

She turned to Kasim. "You get this, right?"

Before he could respond, she launched into it.

"If Dena wasn't the instigator, she was at least complicit in the final act. She killed two people, one of whom was reported to be her. Instead, it most likely was her roommate Melanie. That was her body found in the rubble of the bombed-out building.

"Had she planned it that way," Theo said. "Had she befriended Melanie only to set her up to take the fall? What kind of demon does that?"

"You—we—don't know if that's how it all went down, Theo," Kasim offered. "We do know that she didn't draw this."

"Why do you say that?"

"If she'd drawn this, she wouldn't refer to herself as 'Dena.' She would have written 'Me.'"

Theo nodded. "Flimsy. But, okay. Let's say that's true. Yet, she had it hidden in her purse for a reason. She *knew* what was going down."

Kasim sat cross-legged on the bed, eyes closed, fingers pressed together as he mulled over the evidence.

"Maybe not, Theo. What if the 'X' meant something else?"

"Such as?"

"I don't know," he said, shaking his head.

Theo straightened her shoulders and leveled her gaze. "Okay, I'll give you that. Maybe the 'X' meant something else. What?"

"I don't know. Maybe a piece of office equipment—a copier—a coffee machine—a small refrigerator. Something."

"It was 1979. I'll bet they were still using typewriters—not computers."

"Actually, Theo, years before 1979, Commodore, Apple Macintosh, even Atari were ramping up. The Congressman could have had computers—at least one—in his campaign office. And photocopiers were around. Xerox certainly was. So it wasn't exactly the Dark Ages. I'll bet that diagram was for some piece of equipment that was supposed to be delivered. Because that drawing doesn't put the 'X' on someone's desk, I'd be willing to bet it was a photocopier. They were big and noisy. Putting it in a space, like a break room, wasn't out of the ordinary."

Theo sighed. "Sure. Okay. But why did she hide the diagram in her purse, sewed up in the lining and hidden if it was simply instructions for installing a photocopier? Was it a secret?"

Kasim shook his head. "I don't know."

"I get a different scenario," Theo said, folding her arms defiantly. "How's this: Dena befriends Melanie. They rent an apartment under fake names. Dena gets a job at O'Keefe's office. Dena—or someone—draws a layout of the Congressman's offices and marks the spot—the location of the bomb with an "X." Dena—or someone else—writes the date of the explosion on the same schematic. Dena—or someone else—writes those same numbers on a dollar bill that Dena keeps, in her wallet, perhaps planning to hand it off to someone else—Melanie, maybe—to warn her not to be in the office at a certain time. But for whatever reason—planned or not—Melanie doesn't get the message.

"Then, a package arrives. Maybe it's a gift basket of fruit. Melanie puts it in the break room, next to the Congressman's office.

"But the fruit basket is really a bomb in disguise. Melanie doesn't suspect. Then the explosion happens—on the date and at the time written on the paper that Dena *happens* to have hidden away in her purse.

"Dena learns that the fruit basket is really a bomb. She heads to the office but doesn't make it in time. BOOM! Dena lands on the sidewalk unconscious. Melanie, or whatever her name is, and the Congressman's chief of staff die in the explosion. Do you have a different conclusion to draw from *those* facts? Because if you do, I want to hear it!"

"Look," Kasim said. "All I meant was that this points to the date and time of the explosion. It says that Dena knew something about it. It says that Dena had to be talking to or working with someone else. It doesn't say she intended the results to be what they were."

Theo shook her head. "You're too kind! As far as I'm concerned, this—," she held the drawing in her shaking hand— "this just crossed the line from circumstantial to cold, hard facts, counselor! I think Dena knew all along there was a bomb planted in that office. Oh, and here's a news flash. The mother who deserted me is a stone-cold killer. There. End of story!"

She tossed the paper on the bed, grabbed her jacket and headed toward the door.

"Theo, where are you going?"

"I need some air."

With that, she was gone.

It was nearly 5 p.m. when Theo returned.

Kasim sat cross-legged on the bed. He looked as if he hadn't moved. Theo dropped her denim jacket and scarf on her bed and headed to the bathroom. When she returned, she walked over to the desk and opened a bottle of water. She took a long pull, then recapped it.

"Feeling better?" Kasim asked.

"Yeah." She nodded. "Just needed to blow off some steam."

"Well," he said, "while you were gone, look what I found."

He turned the laptop so she could see. There were columns of what appeared to be names. Theo couldn't make out anything more.

"Okay. I give. What am I looking at?"

"This is the list of patients at the St. Francis Memorial Hospital on February 25, 1979. And that," he pointed to a second column, "is a listing for a 'Jane Doe' brought in. She was thought to have been walking down Mason Street when the bomb went off. She was knocked to the ground and unconscious when they found her. She didn't have any ID on her."

Theo stared at the patient's name. "You think that was Dena?"

"Pretty sure," he said.

"But if they thought she lived in the neighborhood, wouldn't the cops have circulated her photo and asked around? Surely someone would have recognized her."

Kasim smiled. "Exactly. Someone."

Theo drew in her breath. "Rhett! He would have known that was Scarlett."

Kasim nodded.

"He didn't turn her in—."

"Nope. He didn't."

"That's how he knew," Theo said. "That's why he kept her things secret. That's why he gave them Melanie's clothes. He figured the dead girl was Melanie and the cops needed her clothing to match her size. That's why he put Dena's ID in with Melanie's things so the cops would think she died in the blast. He knew all along!"

"Yep."

"He knew she had escaped!" Theo said. "And he wanted her to!"

Kasim was nodding.

"And her purse?"

Theo smiled. "Rhett must have been one of those on the scene after the explosion. Maybe he stayed with her until the ambulance arrived. Maybe he took her purse—as a precaution. Then, when she never came back to the apartment, he figured she was involved. So he kept it hoping she'd contact him. But she never did."

Kasim was nodding in agreement. "And, since we're writing the story from hindsight, I'd say this Jane Doe with amnesia was Dena. Now, look at the hospital transfers a week later. See this—," he pointed to the 'Jane Doe' patient. "She was transferred to a convalescent hospital. I'm guessing she had—or pretended to have—amnesia. If she was out of danger and healing okay, they would have moved her to a convalescent hospital for further recovery."

"Can we access those records?"

Kasim grinned. "Already did."

"And?"

His fingers clicked over the keyboard and another screen appeared. "This is the screen for admits to the Greenbrier Convalescent Hospital in Oakland. It looks as if Jane Doe was admitted under the care of Dr. Tom Seeger. Then, three weeks later, 'Ms. Stephanie Warner' was released. I checked back to see when Ms. Warner was admitted. There's no record of her. I believe—"

Theo jumped in. "Stephanie Warner is Jane Doe alias *Dena Hartsohn*!"

"Bingo!"

"But who was this 'Stephanie'? Is there a home address for her?"

"Hold on, hold on!" Kasim smiled again. "You know, Theo, the Internet is a wonderful treasure chest of useful information. With a Google search, I discovered that a Stephanie Warner married Thomas Seeger, M.D. on June 21, 1980. I also discovered that the Seegers moved around a couple times before Dr. Seeger landed a job at Memorial Hospital in the sleepy hamlet of Santa Maria in San Luis Obispo County. A further Google search of county land purchases shows the Seegers bought property on Blue Bird Lane in the lovely upscale community of Avila Beach. That property has not changed hands in roughly twenty-five years."

Kasim grinned a satisfied smirk. "I'd be willing to bet that if we took a little drive to 8945 Blue Bird Lane and knocked on that door, we might find the answers we're looking for.

"Let's try to get some rest. We'll head out early tomorrow morning."

That night, Theo tossed and turned. Questions she couldn't answer ravaged her thoughts. She dropped off just before dawn only to be awakened, minutes later, by the buzz of her cellphone alarm clock. Groggy, and with a gnawing dread in her stomach, she rolled out of bed and headed to the shower.

15

The medical examiner was pointing to the ugly gash in Mr. Slagg's forehead, just above his left eye. "I don't believe this is the cause of death, detectives."

Detectives Gault and Stern leaned in, taking in the blood-encrusted gash.

The ME continued, "Had Mr. Slagg tripped and fallen, let's say, he might have hit his head on the corner of a table. That's what would produce this type of wound."

Gault said, "His apartment was a slagheap—no pun intended—of decades-old crap. Newspapers, boxes and piles of junk. Small appliances, clothing and other debris, God knows from where. His litter started at the front door and spilled out into every room. Where we found him was at the base of a table with a ceramic tiled surface. There was blood on the corner to suggest that he may have fallen, hit his eye on the corner of table and that was it—lights out. With all the sh—, er, stuff, in that apartment, he could have tripped on almost anything. It was a minefield of crap."

The ME looked at Gault over the rims of his glasses. "Of course, detective, that may have been exactly how he got the nasty laceration here," he said pointing once again to the gash over the eye. "Tell me, detective. Was the victim lying face up or face down?"

"Face up," Stern said.

"Ah. So, if Mr. Slagg tripped or became disoriented, he might have lost his balance and fallen. During the fall, he could have hit the side of his face on the corner of that table. That, alone, however, was not the fatal injury."

Gault stared at the ugly wound. "So, this wasn't what killed him?"

"No," the ME said. "If he tripped and hit his head, he might have tried to right himself—unsuccessfully—and continued to fall, twisting possibly and winding up on his back. That makes sense. However, it doesn't explain how he sustained this."

"If you'll help me here," the ME said, gripping the body by the shoulder and rolling him up away from the metal examining table.

"This was the fatal blow," he said, indicating an indentation that had compressed Slagg's skull just centimeters above the medulla.

Gault and Stern tilted their own heads to study the wound.

"This, gentlemen, could not have occurred by Mr. Slagg's head impacting the floor from a fall. *This* is the result of inflicted blunt-force trauma to the back of the head. My guess is that Mr. Slagg was struck from behind with something roughly ten centimeters—about the size of a heavy flashlight, or the bottom of a heavy vase. That's what propelled Mr. Slagg's head downward and onto the corner of the table. Thus, he was mortally wounded by the first impact. That blow is what caused his immediate death. Had he merely tripped and hit his head on the table, I believe he might have survived the gash to his forehead."

"You're certain?" Stern said.

The ME nodded. "Most definitely. Gentlemen, I believe this was no accident."

Detectives Gault and Stern arrived at the Columbus Motor Inn and were told that Kasim Jabul and Theo

Hunter had checked out very early that morning. The clerk said they'd told him they'd called a cab and were headed to the airport. Gault called police central, gave them Kasim's cell phone number and requested GPS tracking be initiated.

The clerk gave them the keycard to the room and told housekeeping to hold off cleaning it.

Gault and Stern pulled up the sheets, checked the shower, bagging a used bar of soap. They called in a forensics team to lift fingerprints from the bathroom faucets. They gathered used plastic glasses and empty water bottles.

When the call from the technology specialist came, they learned that there was no signal to home in on Kasim's GPS. They figured his cell phone was turned off.

Gault initiated an All-Points Bulletin with photos of Kasim and Theo taken from the surveillance camera log. Sergeant Connors in records saw the APB and called Stern.

"Ah, Stern? You're not gonna believe this. But these two were down here yesterday. They logged in and were going through cold-case files."

"Shit! How'd they do that?"

"They had picture IDs. Took a photo of 'em. Want me to send them to you?"

"Yeah! What files did they check out?"

"They didn't check anything out. Just asked for directions to the really old ones, sixties and seventies. They mentioned something about O'Keefe and that bombing."

"Don't let anyone else into those files. Stern and I'll be there in fifteen minutes."

Gault called his office. "Get in contact with the San Diego police. I want any and everything they've got on these two. Get TSA at the airport and send them those photos. They may be armed. They sure as hell are dangerous!"

Kasim and Theo rented a car and mapped directions to the address they had in Avila Beach. They were two hours into the nearly four-hour drive down Highway 101 when Kasim thought they should check in with Ibrahim. Since Kasim had given Gault his cell number when he and Theo were interrogated, he had a feeling that it would be wise not to use it. Theo placed the call using her phone. That number wasn't on the SFPD's radar—yet. Ibrahim picked up almost immediately.

"Hello, Theo. I am happy to hear from you. How is your search going?"

Theo put the phone on speaker. She and Kasim were a tag-team giving Ibrahim a brief outline of their findings and suspicions.

"You believe Dena is alive, then?"

"We believe she married that doctor using a fake name," Kasim said. We don't know if she's still alive. But we've traced the doctor to an address in Avila Beach in the San Luis Obispo area. We're driving there now. We should know something definite in about four hours. We'll let you know as soon as we've found the house."

Ibrahim responded, but the reception started to crackle. "What's . . . the . . . ?"

Before Kasim could answer, the cell phone dropped the call. Theo said her battery was nearly dead. She switched it off and plugged it in to recharge.

Once they left San Francisco's sprawl behind, the drive down Highway 101 was bucolic. Soon, rolling hills speckled with grazing cattle gave way to vineyards with their crenellated rows of trellised grapevines spilling across rounded hills that were fading from green to gray as the light was softened by fleeting clouds.

Towns and regions still bore the names of the Spaniards whose massive land grants once spanned vast territories. Monterrey, Soledad, and San Lucas played tag with the more anglicized King City, Lockwood, Templeton. Each bearing witness to the many influences that established ownership of the region over the years of conquest and settlement.

Two and a half hours in, they made a comfort stop in King City on the Salinas River. They pulled into the Chevron and topped off their gas tank. Theo was hungry so they stopped in at the Burger King and polished off a couple of burgers. A wall-mounted TV was broadcasting the midday crop reports and news when Theo heard her name. She glanced up at the screen and saw photos from the ID badges Kasim had created for them. She reached across the table and grabbed Kasim's arm.

"Kasim! We're wanted! SFPD say we're persons of interest in the murder of Slagg!"

"Time to go!"

There were only a few others in the fast-food restaurant. A teenage girl, busy texting on her cell phone, and two men in work clothes, chatting in Spanish. The cashier wasn't paying attention to the TV and the cooks were busy working on drive-through customer orders.

Theo and Kasim picked up what was left of their lunch and calmly walked to the waste can and dumped their trash. They headed out the door and got into the car.

"Theo, that's an All-Points Bulletin. That means that by now they figured we're not at the airport. So, they've checked the car rentals and have our car and license plate. Law enforcement up and down the highways will be looking for us."

"What do we do?"

"We need to be off the main road.

Theo reached for her cell phone.

"No!" he cautioned. "We can't turn on our cells. They have my number and by now they probably have yours. They'll be pinging cell towers and use those to track us with GPS."

"Don't they need a warrant or something?"

"Not if we're suspects in a murder. That's probable cause."

Theo's gut wrenched and she hoped the burger and fries she'd just consumed would stay put.

"Look in the glove compartment for a roadmap."

She did. There was one. Theo located their current position.

"Okay," Kasim said. They don't know we're headed to Avila Beach. They probably assume we rented the car to avoid the airports. It's likely they'd think we'll take Interstate 5, which they'll be tracking. They also figure that we might be on 101. That means we need to find an alternative route."

They studied the map, plotting a route using surface streets and California state highways that connected the central coast and US 101 with Paso Robles. Theo's new role was map-reading and navigating while Kasim drove. They eased onto South Vanderhurst Avenue, zigged to Mesa Verde Road, then zagged to Wildhorse Road. After a few miles, they turned onto Cattlemen Road and finally onto CA-198.

"I can't believe they think we killed that old man," she said. "I thought they bought our story about wanting to move to San Francisco and all."

"I don't think that's what tipped them off," Kasim said.

Theo shot him a sideways glance that could melt stone. "I'm guessing the impersonating an officer—correction—*two* officers, was the tip-off."

"We never would have realized that Slagg switched clothes boxes if we hadn't, Theo. And that wouldn't have led me to look at hospital records and we wouldn't be on Dena's trail right now."

"You realize that I am perfectly willing to write her off, don't you? It's bad enough knowing she was involved in those murders. Now, I'm going to have to try to find her and confront her—face to face! I'd rather just think she died. Now I have to live with the knowledge that she's a murderer."

"Murderess," Kasim corrected. "Murder-*er* is male. Murder-*ess* is—"

"Shut up!" Theo snapped.

A few minutes later she said, "Take the next right onto CA-46. We stay on this for 10 miles, then left on Old Creek Road."

They continued winding their way through the hills and valley region in silence. The only words spoken were Theo's navigational directives. Just before dark, they pulled into coastal town of Avila Beach.

"Theo, we need to call Ibrahim and let him know what we've found. He'll be worried about us."

"Where's a public phone when you need one?"

"There!" Kasim said. "There's one outside that bar."

Theo stayed in the car while Kasim fished out enough coins to place a call. Kasim filled Ibrahim in on what he and Theo had uncovered. Ibrahim cautioned Kasim not to confront Dena by themselves. "Let me meet you there. I got on the road soon after your first call. I can be there in about three hours. I'll bring cash. You can leave that rental car and travel with me undetected by the authorities. Do you have enough money to get a room someplace?"

Kasim said that he thought they did.

"Use fake names and call me from the room phone as soon as you do."

"Good. Register under Mr. and Mrs. Sanchez."

Theo and Kasim parked the rental car two blocks from the Mariner's Overlook Motel on Harbor Drive. They registered as Ibrahim had instructed. Once in their room, Kasim used the phone there to call Ibrahim's cell and gave him the address of the motel. Kasim turned on the TV and waited for the afternoon news. Theo turned on her cell phone and mapped the coordinates from Harbor Drive to 8945 Blue Bird Lane. Then, she shut it off. They waited for Ibrahim to show up.

16

While Kasim was busy on his computer, Theo took up the TV remote and looked for something to take her mind off the mess they were in. Turner Classic Movies was showing "The Wrong Man," a 1956 Hitchcock film based on a true story about a man wrongfully accused of robbery and his terrifying imprisonment. Hitchcock's mastery of suspense, his use of light and dark to create ominous shadows foretelling danger, and his famous "whirling camera" technique used to exaggerate being disoriented and lost, was too grotesquely real to Theo.

Instead of a diversion, it intensified her anxiety. She was on the run from the law and suspected of killing an old man. What was possibly even worse, the mother she had never known was taking shape as a callous killer, guilty of two, possibly three murders. Theo's stomach clenched and she couldn't catch her breath. She jumped up and rushed into the bathroom.

Kasim waited until the telltale sounds of Theo being sick subsided. Then he tapped on the door. "Theo? You okay?"

"Yeah. Better." Theo stared at her reflection in the mirror. She knew what it was that she had to do. And she had to do it alone. She splashed cold water on her face, pulled her damp hair back into a pony tail, and opened the door.

"I'm going to the house. I have to see if she's there."

Kasim's eyes widened. "You know that's crazy."

"Hunted and falsely accused of murder—that's what's crazy. What difference does another 'crazy' make at this point?" she said. "We're too close to let a chance to catch this monster slip away. It's time to pay 'Mommie Dearest' a visit."

Kasim simply stared at her, trying to form a counter-argument. Against all the warning signals to the contrary, he understood her logic. He didn't agree with it, but he got it.

"Okay. Then we'll go together."

"No," she said. "You need to stay here to meet up with Ibrahim. He's the only one with credibility at this point. He can clear our names with the police. He said he'd be here in a few hours. It'll be dark soon and the area is rural. No one will pay attention to me. I'll stay in the car and watch the house. I'll wait until you and Ibrahim get there."

"Theo, I don't think—"

"That it's a good idea? I think you could argue that one all day. Save your breath. It's what I'm doing."

"Be careful," Kasim said. "Don't confront her. Wait for us."

She grabbed the keys and was out the door.

From Harbor Drive, just blocks from the beachfront, Theo took Avila Beach Drive and wound through the back roads, overhung with black oak, eucalyptus, and pine. She skirted the San Luis Obispo Creek and golf course, climbing up into the hills with sprawling residential estates smartly situated at bends in the road and bestowed with stunning viewpoints of the bay. Through each well-choreographed S-curve, she glimpsed tiled roofs and metal gates hidden behind dramatic, orchestrated landscapes, botanically tuned so as to blend into the countryside. She crossed roads with names like Fire House Canyon Road, Country Club Drive, and Belleview Orchard Lane. After a few wrong turns, she eventually found herself on Blue Bird Lane and followed it to 8945. She parked a respectful distance from the edge of the driveway that followed a semicircle in front of the sprawling pink Spanish Colonial. She was grateful that the lush landscaping with palms and cascading bougainvillea over the stone wall hid her car from the front windows.

From her vantage point, Theo watched as dark clouds began massing in the west. The weather reports said the remnants of a large Pacific Northwest storm system was heading down the coast and scheduled to hit the area sometime that night. She hoped it would hold off until Kasim and Ibrahim could get there.

It was an hour into her stakeout. The late afternoon shadows had all but disappeared as a darkening shroud of gray descended around her. She had counted only a few cars on the road as the locals returned home from work, play or whatever it was they did to occupy their days. No one seemed to pay any attention to the dark sedan parked beside the road.

Theo figured her cover was working. Before the night shadows completely descended, she pulled out her phone and snapped a few photos of the house. Headlights appeared in the rearview mirror. They slowed. Quickly, she put her phone to her ear, in case the driver wondered who she was and what she was doing parked along a rural road in the upscale neighborhood. The large Land Rover passed her and eased into the driveway. A woman got out, juggling shopping bags, while cradling a cell phone between her shoulder and ear. She headed to the front door.

Theo felt her heartbeat throb into her throat. She swallowed it back and weighed her next move—if there was to be one.

A lifetime of doubts, fears, frustrations, even anger, raged up like bile as Theo watched the woman go about her ordinary routine as if she were just an ordinary person—not a child deserter, killer, and terrorist-in-hiding. She couldn't get a clear look at the woman's face, yet Theo was certain it was Dena.

Then, the woman turned and headed into the house.

Theo's stomach tightened. If she believed that her gut was intuitive, she'd have to go with what it was telling her. Her search was over. She'd found Dena, the woman who was a dichotomy of opposites—the mother who deserted her, the mother who sent money every year to Theo's grandmother for her care—the terrorist who killed innocent people—the killer who murdered an old man who protected her from the authorities for all those years.

"Who *are* you? And how can you live with yourself?"

Theo gripped the steering wheel. She wanted to jump out of the car and confront Dena—to accuse her to her face. She wanted to revile her for what she'd done and for all that she'd failed to do.

"Common sense," she repeated over and over like a mantra. "Stay calm. Wait." Kasim's warning buzzed in her head: *Don't do anything stupid, Theo. We won't be long. Wait for us.*

She checked the time on the car's dashboard. "Ibrahim said he'd be at the motel in a few hours. He should be there by now. It's only a little longer. I can wait. Hell! I've waited all my life for this moment. What's a few more—"

The woman returned to the car and retrieved a couple more bags from the back. She aimed the remote. Car lights blinked as the tailgate started to close. Then she headed in the direction of the house.

Lots of things about Theo's mother's case bothered Kasim. Something about a mother sending payments for her daughter's care all those years didn't jive with the image of a woman dissident-turned-terrorist. Also, something Ibrahim had said to him that day they met in his office bothered him, too.

Ahmed had loved Dena. Ibrahim had said so. He said finding out whether she survived and whether or not she had borne Ahmed's child would mean the world to him. Once he knew that, then he'd be able to connect with his brother's child—or move on. "Like you," he'd said, "I have an emotional tie—a strong one. The heart knows what the heart knows. No one can know more."

"The heart knows what the heart knows," Kasim repeated, drumming his fingers on the computer keyboard. He stared at the screen, trying to relate Ahmed's desertion with the behavior of a man in love.

"If that was true, if Ahmed thought Dena survived, why didn't he try to find her after the explosion? One who loves that deeply would have. And what of his child? Ahmed could easily have estimated a birthdate and checked birth registries in hospitals in the area. Why would he leave the country and go to Palestine to fight if he thought he had a child *here*?"

Kasim couldn't accept Tafiq Ibrahim's excuses for his brother's actions or his lack of caring for the woman whom he loved and their child. Desertion just didn't add up in that equation.

"Something's wrong with Tafiq's explanation," Kasim said aloud. "Did he lie? If so, why?"

Then Kasim did something he had not done in quite some time. He launched his hidden profile web browser and typed in a complicated access code. Within seconds, he was in—migrating through the murky recesses of the dark web's cyberspace, launching an investigation of Tafiq and Ahmed Ibrahim.

17

Theo stared at the middle-aged woman in her jeans, stylish turned-up collar on her denim jacket and short caramel leather boots. Her matching ball cap with just a hint of faded hair pulled through the opening in back and cinched in a ponytail looked casual and chic. Dena aced the role of the perfect, well-heeled suburbanite, socially adept and with time on her hands for crafting a lifestyle that the privileged few enjoy. She didn't look anything like the terrorist who had abandoned her baby daughter and pursued a life of crime decades before.

"How do you do that," Theo mumbled. "How can you kill innocent people and then go on to live your life as if nothing ever happened?" She fumed. "What kind of monster does that?"

She glanced at the clock. Five-thirty. "Ibrahim should be at the motel by now. He and Kasim should be here in about thirty minutes. But what if they're delayed? What if she decides to go out?"

Theo fidgeted. She was antsy. She occupied herself rehearsing what she'd say to Dena. "So, *mother*, what happened thirty years ago? Forget your way home?"

She smirked. "Yeah. That's a perfect opener—sarcasm with a snotty touch of contempt. I like it!"

Theo looked at the clock, again. She tapped her hands on the steering wheel and thought. She thought about all those years in her grandmother's care. She thought about her grandmother's dedication and self-sacrifice. She thought about Dena's abandonment of her baby daughter and her past life while reinventing a new one. She thought about her father's sacrifice, and wondered what he would think of the woman Dena had become. The more the images emerged, the more anger seethed like a vinegar-baking soda lab experiment until it boiled up and over the top of her emotional regulator.

Theo considered the possibility—remote possibility—that the APBs hitting the airwaves with her and Kasim's images and names might reach Dena and send up panic signals.

"All she has to do is switch on the nightly news and get an earful. What if she sees that and figures we're on to her? What if she bolts? What if she escapes—again!"

Theo tossed rational control aside. "Not again! You're not getting away with it this time!" she spat, wrenching the door handle open.

She marched up the driveway to the front door and pressed hard on the bell. Deep, melodic chimes resounded from within.

It wasn't long before the sound of boot heels striking a tile floor echoed and grew louder as someone approached from within. Theo straightened her shoulders and stood erect, wired, ready for whatever or whomever she was about to face.

The door swung open. Theo and the woman stood face to face. Now cap-less, the woman's auburn hair, streaked with grey and loosened from its ponytail, rested on her shoulders.

All the angry words of condemnation that Theo had rehearsed dropped away, unuttered. She stared at what was probably a mirror image of herself in another twenty years: deep-set hazel eyes, creamy skin not yet marred with the signs of age, and wide, full lips that turned up at the corners with soft laugh lines.

If either of them was stunned, it didn't show. There was no widening of the eyes in shock. No gasp or sudden intake of breath. There was just silence and the intensity of recognition between them. For a moment. Then the woman standing in the doorway said, "Theo. *Oh, Theo.* At last."

Kasim's work in the dark web led to useless dead ends. He remembered Tafiq telling him that Ahmed was a student at Berkeley. It would be unlikely that someone with Ahmed's inclinations would allow himself to appear in the university annuals—too risky for his terrorist activities. However, all students had photo IDs taken upon enrollment. But those records were protected. Kasim decided to take chance. He powered up his cell phone and placed a call to his contact in the Engineering College at Berkeley. The call went to voice mail. He left a message.

While he waited, Kasim skimmed the numerous articles about Professor Tafiq Ibrahim, the esteemed educator, the recipient of several science and engineering awards, and a featured conference speaker. He found a biography in a *Times Magazine* written after Ibrahim received the American Society of Mechanical Engineers bronze medal for significant contributions to science though teaching, writing, and professional accomplishments. In it, Ibrahim credited his older brother Ahmed as being his inspiration.

Kasim queried Ahmed Ibrahim. That was a dead end. He remembered Tafiq telling him that Ahmed had traveled to Europe. He wondered if he'd used a different name. Tafiq's middle name was "Nawali," his mother's surname. He entered both Tafiq Nawali and Ahmed Nawali into his searches and was redirected to Wikipedia and an entry about the much-debated, some would say, infamous, *Wrath of God* operation launched by the Mossad, Israel's secret intelligence agency, after the Munich Olympic massacre of Israeli athletes in 1972.

That same year, the Mossad had targeted members of the Palestinian armed militant group Black September and operatives of the Palestine Liberation Organization (PLO) for assassination. Their mission was to kill those who had supported or carried out the Munich attack. The Mossad believed their actions would deter future violent incidents against Israel.

Hassan Kamal, believed to be one of the masterminds, was discovered living in the Paris Latin Quarter not far from the renowned school of engineering and science, the École Polytechnique. Kamal was gunned down in a hail of bullets as he strolled through the park-like setting adjacent to the university campus. A bouquet of flowers and a condolence card was tossed onto Kamal's body—the infamous and feared "calling card" of the Mossad. It read: "A reminder—we do not forget, we do not forgive."

Tragically, three innocent bystanders were caught in the cross fire, an elderly man walking his poodle, a flower seller, and a young engineering student on his way to class. The student's name was "Tafiq Nawali."

Kasim leaned back in his chair. Questions riddled his thoughts: "Why was Ahmed using Tafiq's name? Were the reports wrong? If Ahmed did use his brother's name to escape detection why would he need to? Ahmed's name was never mentioned in the news reports following the congressman's office bombing. The names Ahmed Nawali or Ahmed Ibrahim weren't on the police radar or they would have been in the reports.

"If it was Ahmed Ibrahim who was the engineering student at Berkeley," Kasim said out loud, "easy enough to check."

His phone buzzed. It was his contact at Berkeley. Kasim explained what he wanted.

"Sure, Bro," his contact said. "I can check, but that was a real, real long time ago. I'll have to dig deep. You'll owe me—big time!"

"Name your price. You've got it!" Kasim joked back.

"Stay on the line. I'm in."

The only sound was fingers clicking on the keypad. Then, "Okay. Got it. Sending."

Kasim's email flashed incoming. He clicked on the attachment. The photograph was grainy, but there was no question in Kasim's mind who had been the young man enrolled at Berkeley in 1979. The face staring back at him was thirty years younger, but there was no mistaking the deep-set eyes with the unwavering, somber stare.

Kasim hit speed-dial for Theo. It went to voice mail. Just then, there was a knock at the door.

"Kasim. Theo. It's Tafiq."

18

"How did you know . . ."

Dena looked at her. "How did I know you were *you*? How could I not?"

Every word Theo had been rehearsing for this very moment seemed stuck. Dena's welcome, her openness, were not what she expected. It was as if Theo had simply just popped over for a weekly visit with mom—not the shocked climax to decades of separation.

Dena reached out to touch her shoulder. Theo pulled back.

"Oh, Theo, I'm sorry. I didn't mean to . . . " she hesitated. "I know this must be so strange for you—"

When Theo didn't respond, Dena said, "Of course, you deserve to know."

That's when Theo recovered her voice. "Sorry? Sorry about what? About deserting me all those years? You're damn right I want an explanation. But you . . ." Theo paused, looking around the well-appointed entryway that led to what appeared to be a *House Beautiful* setting for a formal living room. "You . . . "

"Oh, honey, don't."

"Don't? Don't what? Ask the obvious?"

Dena turned and headed into the living room. She motioned for Theo to join her. Theo didn't budge.

Dena slumped her shoulders and sighed. "Please, dear. Please come in."

Theo complied, but stood, rather than taking the chair Dena indicated.

"I know you are hurt. But, believe me, I never meant not to return to you. It's just that circumstances . . . ," she paused, looking away. "Well, something happened and— "

"You mean the bombing?" Theo snapped.

Dena's eyes went wide. "You know about that?" She straightened her shoulders. "Of course you do."

"Kinda hard to hide a bombing where two people— you included—were killed. So, what happened? A miracle? Jesus descend from on high, reassemble the pieces, and raise you from the dead?"

Dena sagged into the chair and buried her head in her hands. "It was awful. Just . . . *awful,*" she said softly.

"Yeah," Theo said. "It must have been hard on you. All those body parts and all!"

Dena looked up at Theo, shock registered in her face. "Oh, my God. You think I did that?"

"Well, you were listed as killed. Yet, here you are. Sort of begs the question. Doesn't it?"

Dena jumped up. "No! No! I did not plant that bomb. I did not kill those people!"

"You might have told someone—like the cops! Like your family. Instead, you disappear—for thirty-three years! You create another identity. You live another life. Who does that? What *innocent* person does that?"

Dena stood and walked toward the hearth. She wrapped her arms around herself and bowed her head. She looked small and helpless in front of the massive stone fireplace. For a moment, Theo almost felt sorry for her.

"And now, there's another murder."

Dena wheeled around. "What? What do you mean?"

"Old man Slagg. You probably only knew him as 'Rhett Butler.'"

Dena's eyes registered shock. "Rhett? What happened to Rhett?"

"Well, when we met with him, he gave us a box of your clothing which he'd kept all these years. That, and a shitload of other stuff. The man was a hoarder. Funny, the stuff in that box was for a woman size 6. The police had a box with what was supposed to be your clothes—only they were a size 10. You're no size 10. He protected you. Now, he's dead."

Dena raised her arm dismissively. "Theo! What happened to Rhett?"

"Someone killed him. Now the cops think Kasim and I did. So, it looks like being a fugitive is a family trait!"

Dena crossed the expanse faster than Theo thought possible for someone her age. She stepped back.

"*Who* killed him?" Dena shouted.

"Well I didn't, if that's what you're thinking."

"Honey, please. Who was with you? You said 'we.'"

"Kasim. Tafiq's assistant. He and I have been tracking—"

Dena's faced went ashen. "Who? Who did you say?"

"Kasim."

"I heard you say, 'Tafiq.'"

"I did. But it was Kasim who—"

"Theo, what does *Tafiq* have to do with this?"

"It's a long story. But, in short, he's the one who recognized me. He told me I looked just like the photo of you in the locket he had. It had belonged to his brother Ahmed. He said that before his brother died, he told him you were pregnant. He wanted to find you—if you were still alive—to discover if it was true. If you had borne Ahmed's child. He had Kasim work with me to find you."

"Theo, what does this *Tafiq* look like?"

"What? Why?"

"Theo, *please!*"

"I don't know. Medium height and weight. Older—your age. Dark hair with grey—just like yours. Beard."

"Do you have a picture?"

"No! What's this got to do with—?"

"Theo!"

Theo thought for a moment. "Wait. Can I use your cell phone? Mine's—er—indisposed at the moment."

Dena gave Theo her phone. She did an internet search for "Tafiq Ibrahim" and several websites popped up. She selected one of the many engineering conference sites and pulled up the list of speakers. Tafiq Ibrahim's name and photo were displayed. She handed the phone to Dena.

At Dena's sudden intake of breath, Theo's thoughts suddenly jelled.

"It's him. Isn't it? This is not *Tafiq*. This is *Ahmed*!"

Dena nodded. "I thought he'd died … in Palestine. That's what I'd heard. I thought I was safe."

Dena's shock turned into immediate action. "Where's Ahmed now?"

"Probably on his way here. He and Kasim—"

"Theo. We're in danger!"

"What?"

"Come on," Dena yelled, grabbing her purse. "We have to get to the police."

Theo followed her out the door. Dena jumped into the Land Rover and signaled to Theo to get in.

Theo balked. "Look, I don't—"

"Get in this car or we'll both be dead!"

Theo did. Dena wheeled out of the driveway and onto Blue Bird Lane, heading toward the town of Avila Beach.

Not ten minutes later, Ibrahim's Mercedes pulled up to the driveway. The front door of the house stood ajar. It took him only seconds to realize that Theo and Dena were gone. A cloud of dust rose in the distance as the big SUV's headlights wheeled around the bend. Ahmed Ibrahim smiled. Then he sped off, following the trail.

The Land Rover came to the stop sign at the end of Bluebird Lane. Highway 49 led west to east. Dena considered heading west into Avila Beach, but the possibility that the local police would probably be at the Mariner's Cafe for dinner break crossed her mind. The fact that Theo told her she had checked into the Mariner's Motel with Kasim made a run-in with Ahmed all that more possible.

She weighed her options and turned east, headed to Highway 101.

"Theo, call your friend. See where he is."

Theo's call to Kasim's cell was answered on the first ring.

"It's Theo. Where are you?"

There was a pause, then Ahmed Ibrahim said, "Right behind you, my dear."

Theo glanced in the side-view mirror and saw headlights in the distance.

"They're behind us!"

"Actually," Ahmed said. "It is I, *alone*. At the moment, Kasim is—how do I say this delicately—somewhat incapacitated. In fact, he may be for eternity!"

"What do you mean?" She screamed into the phone.

"What do I mean? I mean he is dead. It is the price for treachery. Ask your mother."

"Hang up on him, Theo," Dena yelled and punched the accelerator.

"Ah, my dear Dena," Ahmed said. "How I have longed to hear your voice all these years."

Theo clicked the phone off.

"Where are you going? Avila Beach is behind us."

"We stand a better chance if we head to the next town, Theo. Ahmed is dangerous and armed. He's killed your friend. We're next. If we can get to the police in Buellton we might be safe."

Theo considered what Dena was saying and it made sense. But before using her phone GPS to find the next police station, she punched another number in her speed dial.

Alex Thorkensen answered on the first ring.

"Theo! How are you?"

"Alex, I need help. I've got a killer on my tail."

Theo put Alex on speaker and briefed her on the situation. "We may be able to get to the next town before this maniac shoots out our tires, but I doubt it. He's in a Mercedes and steadily gaining on our Rover."

"Theo, are you in a Land Rover? If so, you've got four-wheel drive. Can you go off-road?"

Dena yelled, "Yes!"

"Who's that?"

"Dena. My mother."

If this was confusing information, Alex didn't ask the burning question. Instead, she said, "Good. I've used your phone's GPS to pull you up on radar. Hartford Canyon Road is a side road around the next bend. Tell her to take it. He won't be able to follow unless he has four-wheel drive, which I doubt. It's just a quick detour. It meets up with Avila Beach Drive in about 500 yards. Tell her to get back on it and head east to the 101, then south to L.A."

"But wouldn't we be better off heading to San Francisco?"

"No, you're equidistant between Frisco and L.A. You'll stand a better chance in L.A. I know the Bureau Chief there. Trained him. Besides the Frisco chief is a barracuda. We've had words."

That didn't surprise Theo.

"Alex, how long before we get to L.A.?"

"About three hours. The FBI building is on East Temple Street. Dena, stay on the 101, don't veer to the 405. Traffic is crap on the 405 and it won't get you to the FBI quick enough. From the 101 you've got a straight shot. I'll alert the Bureau Chief and he'll have his agents meet you.

Just curious. What's this guy's name and why are you on his hit list?"

"Long story. Look up Congressman O'Keefe and the bombing of his campaign office in 1979. The mastermind behind it was a guy named Ahmed Ibrahim. He now goes by Tafiq Ibrahim."

"That's a damn long time ago. What sparked your investigation?"

Theo glanced at Dena. "It's—a long story and, it's personal. I'll explain later."

"Got it," Alex said. "Look, even if this guy figures out where you are, you'll have put a safe distance between you. You'll be okay."

Dena saw the dirt road and took it. The Land Rover handled the rutted surface as it was designed to do. The Mercedes' headlights disappeared. They reached the end of the Hartford Canyon Road and jumped back onto Avila Beach Drive as Alex instructed. Within twenty minutes they reached Highway 101. They got on it and headed south to Los Angeles.

19

They were thirty minutes into the drive south on the 101 when Dena placed a call. Her husband answered immediately.

"Honey, where are you. I got home and the door was open and your car was gone. Are you okay?"

"Tom, I'm on my way to Santa Barbara. Abbie needed some things for a sorority dance. She was in such a panic, I figured I'd drive them down to her. I'll just stay the night, then drive back tomorrow. I'll fill you in on the details. Honestly, she's such a drama queen sometimes! Don't worry. I'm fine. Sorry about the door."

There was a brief hesitation on the line, then he said, "Sure. Okay. Don't forget we have the Mitchells' party tomorrow night."

"Oh, that's right. Thank you! I did almost forget! It's a potluck and I said I'd bring hors'doeuvres. I'll pick some up on my way home. See you around noon. Love you!"

Theo leaned back into the plush leather seats. It was the first time since she'd jumped in the car that she took notice of the luxurious interior and state-of-the-art digital equipment. She marveled at her mother's lifestyle. All the years since her mother's disappearance—all that she could remember—Theo imagined many scenarios that might have been her mother's fate. She even considered that she was an alcoholic or drug addict living on the streets of San Diego, or worse, the victim of a serial killer. The one situation she couldn't have envisioned was this: the expensive house, the fancy car, designer clothes, dinner parties. Even her friends needing stuff for some social that she'd drive nearly a hundred miles to deliver and her husband not even blinking an eye at it.

"It comes easy to you, doesn't it?" Theo said.

"What does?"

"Lying."

"You must hate me," Dena said quietly.

"Hate you? No. I just don't get you. I've never been a mother, but I'm pretty sure I wouldn't abandon my child just so I could run off and live a high-end life style. Oh, and something else I'm real clear on. I wouldn't be setting off bombs to kill innocent people."

"Theo, I didn't—"

"Yeah, I know. You didn't do it. You said that already."

"No."

"No what?"

"No. You don't know, dear. And I couldn't expect you to."

"You wanna tell me?"

Dena glanced over at Theo, arms crossed, sullen and brooding.

"You look like your brother when he's pissed off at me."

"I have a brother?"

"And a sister. Tom's interning at San Luis Obispo General; Abbie's at UC Santa Barbara.

"I have a sister named Abbie?"

"It's short for Abigail."

"Yeah, I know. My best friend is named Abby—with a 'y'."

"I know."

Theo swiveled in her seat. "How?"

"Believe it not, Theo, I kept tabs on you. Your grandmother and I were very close. Then, after the awful incident, I couldn't contact her—or you. But I did have a private detective give me regular reports."

"You hired a P.I. to check on me?"

"I had to know you were okay. He was thorough. I know about your work and your amazing achievements. I know about Abby with a 'y' and your other tenants. I even know you're engaged to Frank."

"Was."

"What?"

"Was. I *was* engaged to Frank. He's . . . he's gone missing."

Dena looked over at her. "What happened?"

"He is . . . was . . . undercover. That's all I know. Alex is his handler. She said they haven't heard from him in months. Not a good sign." Theo looked out the passenger window at the darkness stretching endlessly into the distance.

"Don't give up hope, Theo."

"You're a fine one to talk. You're the undisputed queen of giving up."

"Do you want to hear the truth? Or have you already decided?"

"The latter," Theo said, not looking at her. "And I'm good with it."

Dena reached over and tapped the screen on the dashboard. The radio blinked to life with the bright harmony of Vivaldi's *Spring Concerto*. It burst forth in an almost giddy tempo, a stark contrast to the dark, brooding atmosphere in the Land Rover cruising down the highway.

Dena did not attempt further conversation, which seemed to suit Theo.

From a safe distance behind them, Ahmed Ibrahim's Mercedes kept pace, undetected.

Calmer, soothing harmonies played across the airways. As Theo's breathing evened out, Dena glanced over at her. She was asleep. Dena relaxed a little. She thought about Tom, her husband, and wondered how she was going to be able to explain to him who she had been. She thought about Tom, Jr., Ahmed's son. And worried about how Tom, Tom, Jr. and Abigail would handle the truth and how they would judge her and the lie that was her life now.

She wondered, too, how they would react to Theo. And whether or not Theo would accept them all as family. And the nagging fear that pricked behind everything she would have to confess—how they would all be left alone if she couldn't prove her innocence, and if any of them would forgive her the years of deception. Her thoughts traveled across the decades, back in time, to San Francisco, 1977 when she first met Ahmed.

20

San Francisco – 1977

Dena was still suffocating in the empty vacuum of despair after the loss of her husband Jim when she had been summoned to San Francisco. Her mother was diagnosed with colon cancer. There was no hope she could survive. Alicia Hartsohn was in her mid-fifties, but she looked years older. A lifetime of hard work, alcohol abuse, and a deepening depression had taken its toll. She didn't last long.

When she was laid to rest, Dena faced a mountain of debt from Alicia's hospital and burial bills. Alicia's one-bedroom walk-up in a rent-controlled, seniors-only complex was paid up until the end of the month. Alicia's rent subsidy ended then and Dena would have to find something else if she hoped to bring Theo to San Francisco. But before she could, there were obstacles. First, she'd have to get a full-time job, one that would support a single mother with a child. Then, she'd need to work out minimal payments on the debt she inherited. Not insurmountable tasks if she wasn't still trying to pull herself up out of the despair that clouded every thought.

Despite the setbacks, Dena pushed on. She took a part-time job at Caffé Trieste where she had worked during her college days and where she had met Jim Hunter. The Crivellos had welcomed her back, even though they didn't really need another employee. She submitted applications for full-time work in every bank, office building, retail outlet, and restaurant in North Beach. The Crivellos were supportive and put in a good word for her with the landlady at a subdivided row house a few blocks away. It wasn't much, a basement studio, but there was no deposit and she could afford it. It was a start.

One afternoon, as she set coffee cups in front of two customers, she saw a young man standing at the bus stop in front of the café. Her breath caught in her throat—he looked just like Jim. Dena rushed outside. It was insane, she knew, but she just had to see his face. She just had to know that it wasn't him. But she was too late. He boarded the Gray Line. She knew it couldn't be Jim—and yet—as she stood there, watching the bus rumble away, the weight of her desperation bore down on her. She saw the emptiness of her life stretching before her, an endless vacuum without hope.

At that moment of weakness, Dena heard the next bus lumbering toward her. The sound grew louder, overtaking thoughts of helplessness. It was a magnet drawing her in. Pulling her toward blessed relief—oblivion. She didn't need to look in its direction to know it was near. She stepped, mechanically, into the street and into its path.

A passerby saw her and grabbed her just in time. Patrons from the coffee shop rushed outside. One was a psychiatrist. He took control, walked her back inside and over to a side booth. Gently, Dr. Sidney Albrecht coaxed her back from the delayed stress reaction that had been building for the three years since she lost Jim.

"My dear, please come to see me at my office," Albrecht said, pressing his card into the palm of her hand.

Dazed and trembling, Dena explained that she didn't have money for treatment. Albrecht told her that he would see her for free. He explained that he had received a grant from a private philanthropic organization to help servicemen returning from the war. Many were suffering from acute anxiety which manifested itself in what Albrecht called a post-traumatic stress disorder. He called it "PTSD." He said that he believed that the military personnel who had served in Vietnam were sufferers. He also said that he believed it was not only a wartime affliction, but that anyone who had undergone great stress and loss could experience extreme mental anxiety. He told her it was nothing to be ashamed of. He said he could help her.

Dena saw Albrecht nearly every day for several weeks. His therapy was beginning to free her from the feelings of loss and guilt. After six weeks, he referred her to meeting sessions with others, who, like herself, had experienced some kind of trauma. He called it "group therapy." That was where she met Ahmed.

Ahmed, who went by "Ahmed Ibrahim," was one of Dr. Albrecht's student protégés who was tasked to observe the sessions. Over a few weeks, Ahmed and Dena shared knowing looks, stifled snickers, and appeared to be of like mind when it came to listening to some of the group who harped on their difficulties—particularly the ones more content with complaining. They lacked the determination to learn coping mechanisms. A few of these seem to love the attention and weren't shy about grabbing the floor. Dena, however, said very little about the circumstances that brought her to therapy: a trait that Ahmed seemed to find fascinating.

Dena noticed him, too. She was excited when his eyes held hers when she did speak. They weren't exactly flirting, but there was a definite connection—maybe even a spark—between them. Despite the ache in her heart for Jim, the young man with the foreign aloofness and hint of an accent was appealing. Even a brief connection with him made her feel alive again.

Eventually, Ahmed asked her to coffee. Dena accepted his invitation.

"As long as it's not a date," she said.

Ahmed assured her it was "just friends," sharing pleasantries and a little caffeine. He said he'd keep the conversation light.

The "coffee-not-a-date" get-togethers became regular events after each group session. Gradually, Dena shared what had brought her to the brink of despair and how she wound up in therapy. Ahmed comforted her and told her that through it she would become stronger, despite her difficulties. He mentioned how he, too, had faced tragedy. He did not elaborate.

Ahmed kept the discussions light. He spoke of his life in Palestine as the son of a wealthy merchant. He painted an exotic picture of life in the Middle East. He spoke of colorful bazaars, of rich, tantalizing cuisine that had its beginnings in biblical times and before. He talked about family cohesiveness and how he could name his ancestors back to fifteen generations. Then, he told her about his brother Tafiq, whom he idolized. He glowed with pride when he spoke of him.

"Tafiq could add columns of numbers in his head. Father wanted him to become a merchant. But Tafiq loved structure. His dream was to become an architect. He was accepted at École Polytechnique, the prestigious school of engineering and science in Paris. Tafiq fell in love with the city—and its girls!" He laughed.

Ahmed never seemed to run out of funny stories about Tafiq and his romantic antics. Dena loved how he made her laugh—how he made her forget the pain of the past. Little by little, her resilience grew and she began to have hope for the future.

Then, one evening as Ahmed walked her to the doorway of her basement studio, it started to rain. Just a few steps from her door, the heavens let loose with buckets full. They both got soaked through.

"Please, come in," Dena said. "We'll dry your clothes. If the rain doesn't let up by the time you leave, you may take my umbrella."

They draped their soggy jackets over the back of a couple of chairs and positioned them in front of the wall heater. Dena made tea on her hotplate and they settled on the couch to wait out the deluge.

"Are you thinking of going to Paris to see Tafiq during summer break?"

Ahmed leaned back and closed his eyes.

"No, Dena. I will not be traveling to Paris this summer. And I will never see Tafiq again."

Dena's sudden intake of breath signaled that she understood immediately.

"Oh, Ahmed, I am so sorry. I didn't realize. I just assumed that—"

"He was murdered," Ahmed said quietly. Then, he told her the story.

"Tafiq was caught in the cross fire of the Mossad's raid on a member of the Black September as he walked in the park near the university. They killed their intended victim but caught three innocent passersby in the flack. One of them was Tafiq."

Ahmed then gave her an impassioned primer on the politics of the Middle East. He told her how his homeland as he once knew it was no more. He described how the Middle East was erupting in violence. How Egypt, once united with Syria against Israel, did an about-face and signed a peace treaty. This triggered more bloodshed as Israel continued its steady incursion into what had been Palestine. The United States became more involved as its government sought to secure oil treaties. It sided with Israel.

He jumped up from the couch and began pacing as he ranted on about the injustices of war and the tragedies of the innocents. Little by little, Ahmed's anger and desperation took root in the fertile ground of Dena's own despair. She understood that dark place where no hope can penetrate.

Dena rushed to him, took his hands in hers and tried to comfort him. Ahmed stared at her. Then he freed his hands and cupped them gently around her face. "You *do* understand."

With that, he leaned in and kissed her gently on the lips. Dena kissed him back.

"I—," she started.

He smiled. "I want you. I've wanted you since the moment I saw you."

Surprised at the sudden awakening of desire, she pulled back, uneasy.

Ahmed didn't move. He simply stood there and extended his hand. It was an invitation to step up, out of the loneliness of the tomb and into the light of living again. She took the step.

"I only have this couch," she said.

Ahmed unfolded a blanket and spread it on the floor. No words were spoken. They made love tenderly, then again with passion. They slept a few hours. Both awoke almost simultaneously and sought each other again. In Ahmed's arms, Dena's fears melted. She drew strength from him. The will to live returned.

Over the next few weeks, they were inseparable. Ahmed introduced her into his circle of friends, fellow students and others who were active in social movements: anti-war protests, civil rights, feminist and gay rights, environmental issues, and others.

When the call came from Congressman Jack O'Keefe's office manager offering Dena a full-time office job in his re-election campaign headquarters, Ahmed encouraged her to take it.

They had made love and were lying in each other's arms when Ahmed said, "I want you to take that job, Dena."

She was surprised and said so.

"But I thought you hated O'Keefe for his role in U.S. negotiations with Israel."

Ahmed turned on his side and gently ran his finger along the side of her face. "I do. I hate him almost as much as I despise the traitors in my country who would seek compromises that reduce my people to refugees in their own land. Yes. I hate him."

"Then, why should I work—"

He put his fingers on her lips. "Trust me, my love. This is a chance to do something big. You will be in a prime spot to funnel information to us."

"Us?"

"Come, darling, do you think this has all been a game? We have a chance to change the course of world politics. You know my friends. They are dedicated. They are good people. They want peace, too. But before there can be peace, there must be justice."

"You frighten me when you speak this way," she whispered.

Ahmed pulled her closer and kissed her long and with passion.

"Do not think we are talking violence. Absolutely not! But, there is an old saying in my country: 'To guard his sheep, a shepherd must kill the jackal as he sleeps.'"

"That sounds like violence, Ahmed."

"It is a metaphor only. By 'kill' I mean infiltrate and learn his actions. With whom does he meet? Who are his backers. That will tell us where to marshal our efforts. We must bring pressure on what matters to him. Money. Always, it is money."

"The job is just an office clerk. Not his scheduler or assistant. I doubt that I'll learn anything that will help you."

"You will be my eyes and ears in O'Keefe's cave," he said, leaning in and kissing her forehead, then nibbling her left ear. "I assure you, you'll see and hear plenty."

But Dena persisted. "Won't they suspect?"

"We already have a young woman in place. She is a volunteer. She will help you. Whatever information comes your way, use her to get it to us. There will be no visible contact between you and my team. You will not be suspected of anything."

"Now, let's talk about this rattrap you live in."

Dena sat up, suddenly chilled. She pulled a sweater over her nakedness. The conversation unsettled her.

"I can't afford anything more than this! I'm still paying off my mother's debts. I need to save money, not squander it on some fancy apartment!"

Ahmed sat up and placed his hands on her shoulders. "I have money. You have refused my help so far. I have already rented you an apartment—not fancy—but better than this. My friend is in place already. You will move in with her."

Dena cocked her head. "Won't that be a little awkward. For us, I mean?"

"There is a charming little apartment building on Chestnut Street. The unit has sunny rooms that face the street. A real kitchen. And a very special bonus. Two bedrooms."

He slid his hand under her sweater and caressed a breast. "We, you and I, darling, will be very comfortable there."

With his free hand, he slipped the sweater up over her head and tossed it. He pulled her against him and began a rhythmic caress. Dena didn't resist.

A few days later, Dena moved into the roomy two-bedroom flat above the Chestnut Street Gallery. Her roommate explained that Ahmed always gave her cash to pay the rent. Mr. Slagg, the landlord, was nosy, so the young woman gave him fake names from "Gone with the Wind." She was "Melanie Hamilton." Dena was "Scarlett O'Hara." He seemed to like the intrigue and played along.

"Just call me Rhett Butler," he had said.

And that was the arrangement. "Rhett" asked no questions and got his rent on time and in cash.

Dena and Melanie were good roommates. Both were neat, organized, and kept the apartment clean. Melanie was usually gone weekends. Dena didn't ask where she went or with whom. She assumed she had a boyfriend. Melanie's absence gave Dena and Ahmed the privacy they wanted. The arrangement was working better than Dena could have imagined. Not having to pay the rent from her own earnings helped her pay her mother's debts and set some money aside for the other plan—to bring Theo to San Francisco.

Dena's boss, the congressman's campaign director, was pleasant enough and, while she didn't see the congressman very often, she did learn the names of some of his wealthy supporters. As was the plan, she shared that information with Melanie. Dena didn't know where that information went, nor did she want to.

Dena could not believe the healthy, happy state she was in. A few short weeks before, she could not have imagined the joy that glowed in and all around her with Ahmed in her life. Aside from her daughter, he was becoming everything to her. When she thought she might be pregnant, Ahmed was delighted. He pampered her and spoke of their future together. Dena loved him. She trusted him.

On the day that she penned the letter to her mother-in-law Catherine Hunter, Dena could not suspect that her life was about to change forever.

21

They kept to Highway 101 which runs north-south in the valleys between the Outer and Inner Northern Coastal mountain ranges. Reports projected heavier rain in San Francisco, losing strength as it moved over the mountains and down the coast. So far, the storm's cells followed the same path, weakening the further south they drove. The smattering of rain was just enough to wet the roads and dirty the windshield.

Dena's concerns weren't focused on the storm. Ahmed reaching them before they could get to the FBI in Los Angeles was the real threat. She knew what he was capable of.

The Land Rover eased into the Chevron on Lindero Canyon Road in Agoura Hills. Theo woke up.

"We need gas," Dena said. "And I need some coffee. How about you?"

"Where are we?"

"We're about 35 minutes from the 110 freeway. My GPS puts us at 45 minutes from the I-405/I-5 merge, which means we should be at FBI headquarters in an hour. You should let your friend know where we are."

"I'm pretty sure Alex has been tracking us since we left Avila," Theo said, yawning.

"Through our devices, you mean?"

"Yeah. We're on their radar."

Just then, Theo's phone buzzed. "Alex?"

"Just checking, Theo," Alex said. "You two okay?"

"We needed gas and coffee."

"Okay, but don't take long. We've been tracking another vehicle that's kept pace with you since a little south of Avila. We think it's Ibrahim. If it is, he isn't far behind. It could just be a coincidence, but I don't believe in coincidences. He's off the screen right now. Maybe he stopped for gas, too. I suggest you get back on the 101 and aim for Temple Street as soon as you can. You've got about another forty-five minutes. My guy will be waiting. Pull into the underground parking garage. Go to level three. That's where he'll be with the other agents. If Ibrahim is following you he'll be trapped."

"Okay, Alex. Thanks," Theo said. "We're pulling out of the station right now,"

They were back on the 101 and continuing south. Dena watched the road ahead, Theo kept her eyes on the rearview side mirror. She told Alex that traffic patterns behind them appeared to be random.

"Yeah, we're not picking up that same vehicle. Guess it wasn't him. Be careful anyway, though. I'll be back with you when you turn off on Temple," Alex said, then clicked off.

"We need to talk, Theo."

"Sure. Just not now," Theo said, her eyes on the map displayed on Dena's dashboard navigation system.

"Seems like a good time," Dena said.

"Unless you know L.A. streets like the back of your hand, I think we need to concentrate on what turns to take so we don't get lost," Theo said. "I'm not so sure Ibrahim isn't far behind us. Neither is Alex. I want to get to the FBI headquarters before he finds us."

Dena nodded. "Of course. You're right."

"Let's get 'Roving Rikki' on it."

Theo turned to her. "Roving Rikki?"

"I named my car's voice-activated navigational system. Seemed more personal."

Dena touched the button on her steering wheel and "Rikki" responded: "Say a command."

"Navigation," Dena said. "Find an address."

"Find an address. In California," Rikki replied. "Say the city, street name and number."

"Los Angeles, East Temple Street, 2-5-5," Dena announced each number separately.

There was a pause, then Rikki said, "When ready. Press the voice button and say, "Set as destination.'"

Dena complied.

Rikki responded: "Setting destination. Route guidance will start." A map was displayed with the route marked in heavy blue lines and a destination time of forty-five minutes.

Theo smirked. "So, . . . is she accurate?"

"Pretty much. I used to get lost. A lot. Roving Rikki saved my butt."

They continued the next few miles in silence. Roving Rikki was quiet, too. The arrow flashing on the navigational screen kept pace with their travel along the 101 headed south.

It was forty minutes later when Roving Rikki woke up, her voice punctuating the silence: "In two-tenths of a mile take exit 2B. Take exit 2B to Los An-ge-les Street," Rikki enunciated each syllable.

"It's right up ahead," Theo said.

The car slowed and took the exit as directed.

"In one-tenth of a mile make a right turn on North Los An-ge-les Street," Rikki directed.

They were at the stop sign when a car's lights loomed behind them. Theo glanced in the side mirror and caught sight of the grill of the Mercedes. Dena saw it, too.

"He's back!" Theo yelled. "He's right behind us!"

Dena's eyes riveted on the rearview mirror. If she panicked, it didn't show. She gripped the wheel and eased onto North Los Angeles Street. The Mercedes stayed close behind. Theo could just make out the shape of the driver, but not his or her face. Gradually, without telegraphing she was aware he was behind them, Dena pushed the Land Rover. It began to pick up speed. The Mercedes kept pace.

"In four hundred, seventy-five feet, turn left," Rikki said. "Turn left onto East Temple Street."

As the SUV approached East Temple Street, Dena started to slow down. The Mercedes did, too. Dena turned. So did the Mercedes.

"You think he knows we know it's him?" Theo said.

"Yeah. Maybe. I'm just trying not to let him suspect that we do. We need to lose him or put some distance between us before he makes a move. At the next turn, I'll speed up."

"We're getting close. Punch it!" Theo said.

Dena stomped on the accelerator. The Rover shot forward. The Mercedes sped up until it was back on their tail. Then, it rammed the back of the SUV. Not hard enough to activate the airbags, but enough to give Theo and Dena a good jolt.

The big SUV swerved, slid into the gutter, righted itself. Dena punched it again. It sped off. But the Mercedes was accelerating fast behind them. As the SUV approached the next intersection, the Mercedes swerved around them, tapping the bumper.

"Turn right," Theo yelled.

The quick right turn put them on a side street. The Mercedes missed the turn.

"Recalculating." Rikki said.

Theo punched the speed dial for Alex's number. There was a delay.

"Damn! We're in a dead zone!"

The SUV approached the next intersection. They turned left, hoping to get back to East Temple. As the SUV roared down Grand Avenue, Theo's cell chirped to life.

"Theo!" It was Alex.

"Alex, he was behind us. He hit us. But we're still running."

"Theo, I've got you on the grid. You're on Grand Avenue. Heading west. You can double back. Take—"

The phone dropped the call.

Theo glanced at the map on the navigation screen. "Take the next left. We should be able to double back. If I know Alex, she's dispatched help by now."

"Theo, we're turned around. I think we should have gone right."

They were speeding down Grand Avenue when headlights flashed in the rear-view mirror, gaining on them.

"He's back!" Theo yelled. "Take the next turn."

The SUV's tires squealed as it careened around the corner, turning west onto Fourth Street.

"Theo!" It was Alex. "He's tight on your ass. He's going to keep hitting you until your airbags explode. You'll crash. Then, he'll have you. We might not be able to get there in time. You need to ditch that car and get someplace where you can hide."

Theo heard another voice in the background. "Okay. Got it," Alex said.

"Theo, you need to head to Hill Street, it's two blocks away. Dump the car and head into the Metro 417 apartment building. The old LA subway runs beneath it. We've got help dispatched. They'll enter from the opposite end. If it goes right, you'll meet up with the agents. They'll hold him off so you can escape."

The SUV reached the corner of Hill and Fourth. Dena slid it to the curb. In the distance, they could just make out the wail of sirens—they sounded a long way off.

Theo and Dena jumped out and dashed toward the entrance to the Metro 417 building. They sprinted through the double glass doors and over the polished terrazzo floor with the brass inset lettering that proclaimed "SVBWAY TERMINAL BVILDING."

They were in the atrium of the very swank condominium complex. A bank of steel-doored elevators stood to the left. Access required a key card.

On the right, a sign proclaimed "Subway" above stately black-glass double doors. They wasted no time and dashed through them.

22

The shock was immediate. They found themselves in what must have been a foyer that led to the original subway complex, now abandoned and an underground tourist destination of sorts for those who relished tracing the steps of Los Angeles' past. It was the dumpster-diving of un-guided tours, off the popular grid and not for the faint of heart.

"Theo, we're trapped!"

"Alex wouldn't have led us here if we'd be sitting ducks," Theo said, scanning the chipped ornamental plaster molding, the faded paint peeling off the walls, and dangling ceiling tiles. Graffiti-decorated walls surrounded them. Panic gripped her as Theo feared she had misunderstood Alex. She didn't see how this derelict building was going to get them to safety.

Then, she spied the sign with a sketch of a hand and extended finger pointing down a flight of stairs. Lettering proclaimed: "Subway."

"There!" she shouted. "This way."

They sprinted down the stairs. This led them into a huge pillared area. The signs painted on the walls announced "Hill Street," with a long arrow. Then, "Track 5," and "Exit" directing them to the lower tunnel.

Theo reached for her phone. It was gone.

"It must have fallen out of my pocket!" She started back up the stairs. Dena grabbed her arm. "No! He's too close.

The cops will be here any minute. We need to run toward safety and away from him."

They headed down the long tunnel and found themselves in the bowels of the subway, dank, dark, and abandoned. Most of the track had been hauled away over the years. What remained was the decaying remnants of a massive subway system. There was a wall map with a red arrow marking their location: "4th and Hill Streets."

The map indicated a path to the Westin Bonaventure at Fig and Flower Streets.

"We should stay put!" Theo warned.

Dena said, "If he gets here before the cops, we won't be safe. Let's keep going."

They were a good fifty feet into the tunnel when they heard footsteps echoing in the stairwell.

They stopped, listening. The footsteps resounded in the deserted tunnel. "Shhh," Dena whispered. "It's him. He's here and getting closer."

Dena pointed to a door marked "Service Personnel Only," and motioned to Theo to go through it. Theo tried the handle. There was a click. The door creaked open. They slipped through into the blackness.

Theo's breath caught in her throat. Claustrophobia. Theo sucked in air and held it, hoping to stave off an asthma—or panic attack. Dena fumbled with something just inside the door. She found the light switch and flipped the lever. Dim lights lined the wood-sided walls where workmen's hardhats hung on pegs along with various tools and equipment. Dena grabbed a pike with a wooden handle. "Just in case," she whispered.

The weak light helped Theo's claustrophobia a little. Even in the dimness, she looked pale. "You okay, honey?" Dena asked.

"I'll be fine. Let's keep going. He might have heard that door opening."

Dena grabbed a flashlight and handed it to Theo. They saw another door. This opened back into the tunnel. They slipped through as Theo switched on the flashlight. They were deeper into the old tunnel now, a huge cave with earthen sides. They heard the sound of water dripping somewhere and, worse, the skittering of little feet—rats, probably. The vermin were disturbed from their scavenging by the women's presence.

"Rats!" Theo groaned, clenching her teeth. "I hate rats!"

"We'll be through here soon, Theo. Keep that light on our path and keep moving."

They were making some progress when they heard it. A door slamming behind them. Then the measured pace of solid footsteps gaining on them.

"Keep the light low to the ground, Theo . . . keep moving."

When the footsteps behind them stopped, so did they. Theo tried to grip the flashlight but her hand was sweaty, clammy, and trembling. She grabbed it with both hands, trying to steady the beam.

"It's no use." The man's voice penetrated the dark, echoing off the walls. He was close. Too close.

"I doubt if you can outrun a bullet."

"Keep going," Dena whispered.

The loud report of gunfire stopped them as a bullet whizzed past their heads and gouged chunks of dank earth that exploded around them.

"I won't miss next time," Ibrahim shouted.

"The cops will be here any moment!" Theo shouted.

"Perhaps," he said. "But by the time they find you, I'll be gone."

"They know who you are, Ahmed," Dena yelled. "They'll get you."

When he spoke, Theo could tell that he was much closer than before.

"No need to shout, my dear. I am right here."

Theo flashed the light on Ibrahim, hoping the flash would blind him momentarily, giving them time to run deeper into the tunnel.

"Don't!" he shouted. "I'll shoot. I'm certain the bullets will strike one of you—maybe both of you."

Dena grabbed Theo's arm. "It's no use. He's right."

Ibrahim moved closer. "There, that's better. The better to see you both."

"It's over," Theo said. "Cops, FBI, the whole damn L.A. police force is on its way. Don't make it worse than it is."

"My dear, you simply don't understand. There is much at stake here. My reputation, for one. After you are dead, I'll escape. I have a passport, a new name, and a new life ahead of me—I'll start fresh, elsewhere."

"Reputation!" Dena spat. "You murdered those people, Ahmed. How could you?"

"You could never understand, my dear. I tried to show you. I loved you. But you . . . you have that ridiculous American concept of fair play, following the rulebook. So naive. I know only justice."

"You call that *justice*? What you did? And you didn't even kill your intended target. O'Keefe survived!"

"The folly of war, Dena. Collateral damage. That old man is living in his own demented hell now. There is justice after all," Ibrahim said with a low, dry chuckle.

Theo spoke up. "Did you kill Slagg?"

"Ah. Well. Yes. He was useless. But he remembered me. That was a problem. He didn't suffer."

"You're a monster!" Theo shouted.

"No, my dear. I'm not. I am the hand of righteousness. That's all."

"And what about Kasim? Is he in on this with you?"

"Unfortunately, Kasim lost sight of the goal. He fell in love. Always a mistake. I would know."

"Where is he?"

"Doesn't matter, really. Does it?" Ibrahim said. "But to answer you, he's dead."

"Why?" Theo shouted. "Why kill him?"

"This is tiring, Dena. She is so much like you. So many questions. I fear I won't be able to answer them. I must get this done."

The sound of a bullet being ratcheted into place resonated off the tunnel walls around them.

"Wait!" Dena shouted. "Don't harm her. It's me you want to silence. Take me with you. I'll go. You had feelings for me once—or so I thought. I'll go with you, Ahmed. I'll stay with you. Kill me if you must, but leave her."

"Really? That's your offer?"

"She has nothing to do with us, Ahmed. Let her go."

"She knows too much, Dena. I simply can't have that. You understand. I can't imagine you don't remember how my mind processes, my dear. I don't suffer problems. I eliminate them."

"What of your son?" Dena said quietly. "Will you kill him, too?"

If this news startled him, he recovered quickly.

"Ah, I wondered if it were true. If you really were pregnant. I doubted it. Perhaps I should have believed you, my dear. I could have searched birth records around that time. Perhaps I would have found you myself."

"He doesn't know, Ahmed," Dena said. "He doesn't know about us or that you—"

"That I am his father?"

"No."

"More's the pity, my dear. Does he look like me?"

Dena tried to keep the conversation going—buying time, hoping the police would arrive before Ahmed shot them both.

"He has your eyes," she said.

"Of course. I will find him."

"Hey, Ibrahim," Theo shouted. "Since I'm dead anyway, tell me this. Was Dena in on the bombing? Did she know about the schematic?"

"Schematic? Ah, the sketch," he said.

"Yeah. That one. Did she know?"

"My dear, Theo. It was such a long time ago."

"Did she?"

"What are you talking about?" Dena blurted.

Ahmed chuckled. "You found the sketch in her purse. Sewed into the lining! I'm impressed, Theo. What a clever girl you are. You could have been my protégé. Sad, now I have to kill you."

"What are you talking about?" Dena yelled, again.

Theo spoke up. "There was a sketch of the Congressman's office showing where the bomb was located. It was on paper and sewed into the lining of your purse."

"My purse!"

"She doesn't know, Theo. You have your answer."

"What sketch?" Dena asked, again.

"Sonja, you knew her as 'Melanie,' and I both knew you wouldn't go along with our plan. So, we used your purse, the one with the blue-glass tassel, as a way to smuggle information between us. We put little notes in a ripped seam and sewed it up. We did that for several weeks. You never caught on, my dear Dena. The last note was the sketch with the location of the bomb and the date and time it was set to go off. It was marked with an 'X'—all very cloak and dagger, don't you think."

Theo piped up: "Did you plan to kill 'Sonja'?"

"Of course not," he snapped. "Sonja wasn't supposed to be there."

"You planned to kill me—even after you knew I bore your child?"

"So *American*, my dear. You are so full of apple pie. You wrap yourselves in red, white, and blue bunting and wear it like a shroud. It smothers you from the real world. You have no concept of revenge.

"Look at that stupid war and every incursion since then. Your husband died for nothing. *Nothing!* Do you really believe that anyone outside your world believes in the Constitution? The Bill of Rights? What rubbish. I have to admit that it sounds so romantic. But it's gibberish. The idea of fairness and justice for all—seriously!

"In the real world, the world where the road meets the rubber—in that scenario, you take your licks and rise up fighting. If you lose, you regroup, then take back. That's how it really works. It's the Old Testament. Not the 'turn the other cheek' Jesus-speak with weak platitudes that don't stand up against your enemies."

"You're sick," Theo yelled at him.

"Perhaps. But I'm not dead—which is what you're going to be."

Dena said, "You would have killed me, even as I bore your child? You *are* a monster."

"You can always tell him that I was a freedom fighter. Oh, wait, I guess he'll never know. Maybe my blood will course in his veins and he'll come to realize who and what he really is. Not an insipid turn-the-other-cheek weakling; but a real man. Someone who takes a stand for what he believes. A real man takes back what is his right.

"But you want the truth, Theo. Well, the truth is that I loved your mother. But sacrifices must be made. I realized she would never go along with the plan. So, I worked around her."

"You planned for me to die in the bombing," Dena said.

"No. I did not. Sonja got the bomb in place. She was supposed to get out. But, things didn't work right.

"You were not supposed to be there. That's why I tried to make you late that day. Remember? We made love again—and again. I didn't want you near the building. But you valued your job over me. So, I let you go. But the delay was enough. You didn't get inside before the bomb went off. I saw them swarm around you on the sidewalk. I couldn't even get close before they whisked you off in the ambulance.

"I went to the hospital but couldn't get near you. Then, they moved you to another hospital. I tried to find you. It was as if someone wanted to keep you hidden. The police? Anyway, I lost you after that. I believed for some time that you died. I mourned you. It is said that truth will out. Later, I began to sense that you might still be alive and in hiding. I tried for years to find a clue, but there was nothing. You simply vanished into thin air."

"I only got a concussion and temporary memory loss. By the time it all came back to me and I figured out what happened, what you did, Ahmed. I couldn't live with knowing that I was involved. I never wanted to see you again. I banished you from my life. I tried to move on."

"And, so you did, my dear. Husband. Family. Nice house. New life. You deserved it. But, then, so did I. I've made a name for myself—I'm someone of importance, too. And now I have to give that all up. Start anew in a new land. My reputation is destroyed and all because of someone who deserted me. That's why you have to die. That's why you both have to die."

"How can you say I deserted you?" Dena said, stalling. "You used me. You are the one who killed innocent people! You did to them what the Mossad did to your brother Tafiq. How can you live with that?"

"Don't speak of Tafiq, Dena! I defended his honor!"

Dena inched closer. "Defended his honor? Is that what you call it? You shattered innocent lives and you think that is love." What is it, Ahmed? Justice? You're insane."

Ibrahim stepped away from the wall. Theo could just barely make out his form. Darker black against a gray black. That's when two things became immediately apparent to her: Dena had positioned herself between her and Ibrahim, and Dena still had the long-handled pike.

"You were always so high-minded, Ahmed. I trusted you. It was you who gave me hope when my whole world fell apart. You were the one who taught me to live again. You were my rock. I . . . ." She hesitated as she inched closer to him. "We were lovers—at least *I* was in love. And we have a son!"

"Stop!" Ibrahim hissed. "Don't speak to me of love. You deserted me!"

"You betrayed *me*!" Dena shouted.

"Lovers can be the most cruel," Ibrahim said softly. "We never forgive . . . we never forget . . ."

Ibrahim was still talking when Dena swung the wooden pike in his direction. "Run, Theo!" she shouted as the pike clipped his arm.

There was a flash of light as the gun exploded.

Dena went down. She was hit. Theo hesitated.

Dena screamed, "Run!"

Theo darted further into the tunnel. Ibrahim's footsteps echoed behind her. Up ahead, she saw the pale hope of a light. She prayed it was help coming her way. She wanted a miracle.

Ibrahim fired. The shot slammed into the side of the tunnel. Clods of earth pelted her. She stumbled, but kept running. The mouth of the tunnel was coming into view. She heard voices.

"Help!" Theo screamed.

"Hit the ground!" came the reply.

She did.

"Drop your weapon, Ibrahim. It's over!" The man's voice boomed toward them.

Ibrahim stopped.

Suddenly, powerful lights flashed around him.

"Drop it!" came the shout again.

Ibrahim stopped. "You see, Theo. This is how it always ends. Love is the killer. Always."

He raised the gun at her.

A single shot rang out.

Theo recoiled as the bullet slammed into her.

Her insides turned to ice. Shock took over.

She was vaguely aware of sinking into the ground, the distant explosion of gunfire all around . . . voices . . . then . . . oblivion.

23

The EMT slid the oxygen mask into place.

Theo pushed it aside. "Dena . . . he shot her . . . ."

The stretcher was hoisted into the back of the ambulance. Clipped voices shouting numbers and words that sounded like a TV medical drama shot staccato-like all around her: "BP - 110 over 100. RR - 40. SPO2 – 72 percent. We need to get her to surgery!"

The guy attending to her said, "The woman's in the next ambulance, Miss. She's alive. Right now, we're trying to keep you that way. Keep this on you until we get to the hospital."

Theo's hand shot up, pushing the mask away again. "You have to help her. She's . . . she's my mother."

"Yes. Yes, Miss. She's on her way to the hospital—just like you."

Theo glanced around at the equipment and monitors, the saline bag hanging overhead, the sights and sounds from inside the ambulance, the siren screaming, as they barreled toward Good Samaritan Hospital.

"I was shot."

"Yes. But you're going to be O.K. Just keep this mask on, please."

Theo nodded that she would. Then, everything went black.

It was spring. Or, it felt like it. She was in a park, on the swings.

"Higher, Grammie! Higher!"

Hair flying about her face as she flew up, then back, Theo squealed with delight.

"I'm flying! I'm flying!"

Suddenly, the woman reined in the swing, pulling Theo from it.

"Come on, Sweetheart. It's time to go."

"No! Grammie! No!" Theo cried in her toddler's voice. "More. Pleeeeeese."

She tried to keep up with the woman running ahead of her down the long corridor and into the blinding light that swallowed everything around her. Her grandmother disappeared.

"Wait for me, Grammie. Wait . . . for me," Theo called out.

"No …Theo … not now," came her grandmother's voice. "Go back."

Then, she awoke.

She was in the hospital and aware of the monitors beeping. She studied the blood-pressure reading: 120 over 80. It was normal. At least she thought that's what normal was.

She raised her left hand. An intravenous tube was attached to the back of it. Her right arm was immoveable. She knew. She'd tried to move it and it hurt.

A remote, its cord wrapped around the bed bars, was in reach. She pushed the "call nurse" button.

Within minutes, a young man in blue scrubs appeared. He was smiling.

"Well, hello, Theo. I'm Charlie. I'll be your server today!" he said.

"Is this any way to treat a customer?" Theo croaked through cracked lips.

"They said you'd be tough. Glad to see they were right."

"They? Who's 'they?'"

"Your peeps, Theo. Your friend Abby. Your boss. Your other friends Oren and Guy. Honestly, they're camped out in the waiting room. One word from me and they'll be here in a hot second. I just need to know if you're ready for that."

Theo gave him a weak movement that looked like an attempt at a smile. "Please, let them know I'm awake."

Charlie disappeared and within minutes Abby strode in, followed by Sam, then Oren and Guy.

"Hey, Chickie. How're you doing?" Abby said, softly and totally out of character.

"I'm fine. Except I can't move my right arm."

"Yeah," Sam interjected. "And you've got the bullet hole to prove it."

"Hi, sweetness! We brought you flowers and See's candy—nuts and chews—your favorite," chirped Oren.

"Hi, guys," she said, mustering up a little cheer. "It's good to see you."

"Hell, honey," Oren crooned. "As far as we're all concerned, it's good to be seen *by* you!"

Abby glanced at the beeping monitors, then back at Theo. "These look promising."

Theo nodded.

The TV was on. The evening new broadcast started by proclaiming "Breaking News."

Abby turned up the volume.

"The decades-old bombing of San Francisco Congressman Jack O'Keefe's office in 1979 has been solved with a bizarre shooting in Los Angeles. Renowned engineering lecturer and professor at San Diego State Tafiq Ibrahim was killed in a hail of bullets. Ibrahim is suspected of being the mastermind behind the 1979 bombing of

O'Keefe's re-election campaign offices where two of his staffers were killed.

"After more than thirty years in hiding, Dena Hartsohn, a well-known socialite now living in Avila Beach, and under an assumed name, has come forward. Through Ms. Hartsohn's testimony, police and FBI have pieced together the astonishing story of a terrorist cell operating in 1979 in San Francisco. Hartsohn's is a tale of fear, intrigue, and fake identity. While details are still being unmasked, what we have learned is that the FBI has solved a decades old crime and unraveled a story worthy of a Hollywood melodrama."

Dena's photograph flashed on the screen along with Ibrahim's.

Theo felt sick to her stomach. She managed to grab the plastic barf dish and vomited into it.

Abby disappeared and returned so fast that she could have been on skates. She produced a damp towel and dabbed at Theo's mouth. Then she offered her the glass with ice chips. "Here, honey, suck on these. It'll help with the nausea."

"Abby," Theo managed to say, "where's Dena?"

"She's here, honey, in this hospital. On another floor. She survived the gunshot. She's going to be okay."

"I've got to see her, Abs. I've got to talk to her. I've got to tell the police what Ibrahim confessed to. Dena had nothing to do with the bombing. They can't charge her with those murders. That report . . . her husband and kids—they'll be devastated when they hear all that."

"Honey, it's okay. The police and the FBI know. They got it from the horse's mouth. Ibrahim confessed before he died. Dena's in the clear."

Theo leaned back into the pillow. Relief spread over her like a clean white sheet on a sultry night.

"Good," Theo said nodding. "Good." Then she slipped into oblivion.

The room was dark when she awoke. Shades of night beyond the window were punctuated by the glimmer of lights from a tall office building in the distance. She was momentarily confused. Then she remembered she wasn't in San Diego. She was in a hospital in Los Angeles. She had been shot. Theo's breathing came in short gasps. She struggled to gain control. She hit the call button.

"Need something?" The nurse's voice crackled over the intercom.

"I . . . I can't catch my breath!" Theo gasped.

Abby, asleep in the chair, awoke. She immediately elevated the head of the bed.

When the nurse showed up, Theo's breathing was evening out.

The nurse checked her vitals. "What happened?"

"I don't know," Theo said, her words labored and interspersed with the effort to take longer breaths. "I woke up . . . I . . . it was unfamiliar. I forgot I wasn't in San Diego. I guess I was just confused."

"You still need to rest," nurse said, injecting something into the IV. "This will help you sleep."

Morphine took over. Theo's breathing evened out. A wave of comfort washed over her. Abby was by her side.

"Hi, Abs."

"Hey, yourself," Abby responded.

Then she remembered Frank. "He'd be here if only . . . if only . . . he were still . . . "

She drifted off to sleep.

Theo slept through the rest of the night.

The light grey of morning filtered in through the curtains. Theo glanced over at the chair. Abby was gone.

The door swung open and a shaft of light from the corridor sliced into the room. The morning shift was on duty.

"How're you feeling, Theo?" the nurse, a tall blonde, asked.

"Like I've been shot. How long have I been out? You're not Charlie."

"You've been sleeping for a while. That's a good thing. I'm Darcy, by the way. Charlie will be back tomorrow. Same time. Same station.

"Your doctor will be in later this morning if he doesn't have surgery. He'll explain everything. It probably feels a lot worse than it is, if that's any consolation."

"Yeah. Good to know."

"You think you could eat some breakfast?"

Theo shook her head "no."

"You need to start getting something into your stomach. How about Jell-O or sherbet?"

"Sherbet."

"I'll get some and be back in a minute."

The nurse was gone when Abby showed up.

"Hey. You're awake.? How're you feeling?"

"Nurse asked me the same thing."

"And?"

"And I told her I felt like I'd been shot."

Abby smiled. "I see you're your usual snarky self. Good sign."

"She's bringing me some sherbet."

"It might be awhile before you chow down on a good T-bone, although I could sure use something. I'm starving."

"Where are you staying?"

"Here."

"Oh," Theo said. "I wondered if you and Sam and the guys came up together."

"No. We drove separately. They just wanted to be here when you woke up. Sam had to get back to the office."

Theo nodded. "Who's watching Bailey's while you're on vacation?"

"The new guy. He's good. He'll be fine."

"How's Dena? I'd like to see her."

"I'll check with the nurse. Not sure if she's up to visitors yet."

"How bad was it?"

"The good news is that Ibrahim was a lousy shot. The not-so-good news is that he managed to nick her in the left thigh. Hit an artery. She could have bled out if the EMTs didn't get there when they did."

Theo nodded. "Is her husband here?"

"Yeah. He's doing the bedside-hotel-stay, too. Him and her kids."

"Did you meet them?"

"Yeah. He's nice, Theo. The kids are, too. Abigail looks like you. They're anxious to meet you. They peeked in while you were out."

"Oh! I look like hell!"

"Funny. That's what *they* said." Abby smirked.

"Thanks. Your bedside manner sucks."

"You'll get to meet them later this morning. I'll call makeup, your highness. We'll have you coifed, painted, and ready for your close-up."

"I'd throw a pillow at you if I had a right arm."

"You'd miss—like always!"

The nurse breezed in with sherbet. Theo tasted it and managed a couple of spoons-full.

"Thanks. That's about it, I think."

"It's a good start," the nurse said. "I'll order a light lunch tray. We'll see if any of that works. The sooner you can get some food in you—and keep it down—the sooner you can get outta here."

"Abby? Did you hear anything about Kasim?"

"I didn't. Alex probably did, though. She said she'd call tomorrow; that was yesterday. So, given the three-hour time difference between D.C. and L.A. I suspect we'll hear from her in an hour or so."

"I can't believe he was in on this with Ibrahim. We would never have found Dena if it wasn't for Kasim."

"If he learns what Ibrahim did and that he's dead, he may be long gone," Abby offered. "I'm sorry he misled you, Theo."

Theo leaned back into the pillows. "I just can't believe . . . after all we went through . . . that Kasim . . . would have . . . hurt me . . . "

Soon, she was dozing again.

24

Sunlight filtered through the sheers that had been drawn across the window to soften the glare. Theo lay there watching it and feeling that clarity about so many things was just as veiled as the window and its view. She glanced over at the chair, but Abby wasn't in it. She figured she'd gone in search of some coffee.

Her door swung open. She expected Abby and was surprised when a tall, dark-skinned man in scrubs breezed in.

"Good morning, Theo. I'm Doctor Rab. How're you feeling?"

"Like I told everyone who asked, 'Like I've been shot.'"

Doctor Rab smiled, "Of course you do—as you should. But I want to distill any fears you may have about your condition. First, yes, you were, indeed, shot. It was a small caliber bullet, a 22, so the damage was much less than it could have been."

Doctor Rab held an X-ray up to the light from the window. "Apparently, the bullet did a clean pass through the flesh just below your armpit. It did not hit bone or any critical organs. It did make a nasty gash, though. You'll have a scar. It will heal, but it will definitely be sore for some time. You will have some restricted movement. Eventually, you will probably gain full use of that arm."

"Looks like I was lucky."

"Oh, my dear, you were most certainly lucky. If I were you, I'd buy a lottery ticket."

"If I were a gambling gal, I would."

Rab tucked the X-ray back into the file. "I want you to stay put for a couple more days. I've got a therapist coming in to start you on some motion therapy. Then, you're free to go. You live in San Diego, right?"

"Uh-huh."

"I've got some referrals here to doctors in San Diego who can take over your recovery. I urge you to work with them. Bullet wounds do so much damage. You'll need therapy—physical and emotional. What you've been through is traumatic on so many levels. You need professionals to turn to when . . . when you feel anxious."

"Anxious? You mean like PTSD?"

"Yes. I mean that. Exactly."

Theo took a deep breath.

"Dr. Rab, do you know anything about my . . . about Dena Seeger's condition?"

"I was not the attending physician when Mrs. Seeger came in. However, I understand she is your mother?"

Theo hesitated only a second. "Yes. She is."

"I'll have the nurse give you her room number. You can call her. But, I'd really like to have you up and moving. So, you can go visit her if you wish."

"Thank you, Dr. Rab. I feel better knowing what I'm dealing with."

"You will be just fine, Theo. You were lucky. Oh, and I'm serious, buy that lottery ticket!"

He turned to leave. Theo said, "Dr. Rab, what's your real name?"

"It's Rabathakian."

"Thank you, Dr. Rabathakian. Thank you for what you did."

Nurse "Charlie" arrived with Theo's breakfast: dry wheat toast, cream of wheat, and black coffee—decaf.

"This isn't very exciting."

"No," Nurse Charlie said. "But it may keep you from upchucking."

Theo nibbled on the toast, took two almost-spoons full of the cereal, and sniffed at the coffee.

Abby arrived with Starbucks—two French Roast Ventis.

"Hey, Gimp, how about some French Roast?"

"Oh," Theo simpered, "you are a lifesaver!"

Theo and Abby were savoring their coffee when there was a knock on the door.

"Hello? May we come in?"

Tom Seeger, Tom Jr., and Abigail entered and stood at the foot of Theo's bed. Tom spoke first. He introduced himself and then the others. Then he said, "Your mother hasn't stopped asking for you, Theo. Are you up to a visit. We're here to help."

Theo looked from Tom Sr. to Jr. to Abigail.

"You know?"

Tom Sr. spoke up. "Oh, yes! We are so excited, delighted and happy to meet you, Theo."

Theo looked at each one of them, "It's been a long journey."

"Yes," Tom Sr. said. "It has. But, it's over now. We are finally together. After all these years. We are family."

Theo stared at them—unsure how to respond or how to feel.

"The FBI . . . "

"Yes, we know," Tom Sr., said. "They've told us that Dena has been cleared of all charges."

Theo sighed and nodded, relieved. "I'm so glad to hear that. I can testify . . . "

"You won't need to, Theo. They have what they want. Dena is free. So, how about that escort? You feel up to it?"

Her stomach did a flip-flop, followed by a wave of nausea. She couldn't catch her breath. She went grey. Theo's eyes darted around the room and found Abby.

"Abby . . . I . . . "

Abby got it instantly. "Tom," she said. "I think Theo is just a little exhausted. Her doctor was in this morning and she's had a lot to absorb."

Tom Seeger nodded, "Oh, of course." Then, turning to Theo, "You get some rest. Here's Dena's room number. We'll be there. You call us when you're ready and we'll come to you. We'll take you to her."

The Seegers were funneling through the door when Abigail turned. "I can't imagine what you're going through, Theo. But, I want you to know. You're family. Besides, I've always wanted a big sister!" With that, Abigail flashed a smile and a wink, closing the door behind her.

The moment they were gone, Theo turned to Abby in a panic.

"Abby! I can't! I simply can't!"

"It's okay, Theo. You don't have to do anything. Not right now. It's okay."

Theo leaned back against the pillows. "Oh, Abby, am I awful?"

"Look, honey. You've had your whole life to wonder about what happened to your mother. You've had a very short few days to come face to face with the answers. It's a lot to take in. You are fortunate. Your mother and her second family want to embrace you. That's the good news. The flip side is that you need some time to work it all out in your head—and in your heart. I have a very good feeling about all of this. And, the best part, I think you are totally up to the challenge. You just need to get through the healing part first. The mental part will follow. It may even lead the way."

Theo's nausea subsided. Her breathing began to even out as some color returned to her face. "You think so? You think I can handle this?"

"Kiddo, I *know* so!"

"I want to take a nap."

"Okay. You rest. I'll go see the family and let them know you're resting. We'll talk about this later."

"Okay, Abby. Later."

After Abby left, Theo tried to relax but she couldn't banish the anxiety that had overtaken her. Sleep alluded her. Finally, she called the nurse.

"I'm really in some pain."

"Sure," Nurse Charlie said. "I've got something for that. Are you still nauseated?"

Theo shook her head.

He left and returned shortly. He injected the IV with morphine. As the opiate coursed through the tube and into her bloodstream, relief was immediate. Her breathing evened out. She closed her eyes and thought of nothing—not the Seegers, not Dena, not Ibrahim and Kasim, and last, but not least, not even Frank. Soon blessed oblivion took over.

25

It was mid-morning when Theo awoke. Voices outside her room got her attention. One of them was Abby's.

"She doesn't know," Abby said. "This might not be the right time to tell her. She's still dealing with the shock of being shot."

The male voice said, "We'll go easy on her. But my instructions are to find out as much as we can about what she does know."

Theo pushed the "head" button on the remote to raise that part of the bed.

"Abby?" she called out.

Abby stepped into the room.

"Did we wake you?"

"What's going on?"

The tall man in a dark business suit stepped around her and approached the bed.

"How do you do, Miss Hunter. I'm Agent Aubrey of the FBI. Are you up to answering a few questions?"

Theo nodded. "Sure."

Abby said, "Honey, if you're not up to this just tell us."

"It's okay, Abs. I'd really like some coffee, though. I'm feeling a little fuzzy."

"I'll get you some and be right back," Abby said, heading out the door.

Agent Aubrey pulled out a small notepad. "Okay, Miss Hunter . . . "

"Theo," Theo said. "Please call me 'Theo.'"

Aubrey smiled. "Okay then, *Theo,* let's see . . . when did you meet up with Dena Hunter?"

"It will be easier if I start at the beginning."

Theo gave Agent Aubrey a *CliffsNotes* version of how it was that she came to be on the quest to find Dena. Aubrey listened intently with minimal questions and a few raised eyebrows when she detailed Kasim's hacking that resulted in fake SFPD ID's that got them into the evidence room at police headquarters. When she got to the escape down the LA subway tunnel she stopped, surprised at the sudden tightness in her chest with the memory of her terrified dash and final confrontation with Ibrahim. The flash of light from Ibrahim's gun, followed by the explosion blasted through her thoughts, obliterating everything else.

It was at that point that Abby came through the door with coffee in hand. Theo threw up her left arm, shielding herself. Abby stopped.

Aubrey was well-acquainted with the reaction. "Theo," Aubrey said softly. "It's all right. You're safe. It's just me and Abby. We're here for you."

Theo lowered her arm. Her eyes darted first to Abby, then to Agent Aubrey.

"I know hospital coffee sucks," Abby quipped. "But I didn't think it was that bad."

Theo stared, then snickered a feeble, nervous laugh.

Abby set the coffee cup down on the bedside table. "This one's got cream and sugar—it's a hospital version of an almost-latte."

As she turned, Agent Aubrey murmured, "Good save." Abby winked.

Theo gingerly sipped the hot concoction.

"Not bad, actually."

They took a few minutes to joke and complain about hospital food. The tension of moments before was ebbing.

Theo cleared her throat. "Okay, Aubrey, I think you know the rest of the story."

Aubrey nodded. "Your story pretty much corroborates what Mr. Jabul told us."

Theo's eyes widened. "Kasim? You found Kasim?"

"Yes. He's at the hospital in San Luis Obispo."

"The hospital? He's alive?"

"Apparently, after you left for Dena's house, Kasim did some research on Ibrahim, something he never bothered to do before. He put the loose ends together and figured out that "Tafiq Ibrahim" was really "Ahmed Ibrahim Kawali" and that he had assumed his dead brother's identity after the bombing. Kasim guessed that Ahmed was the mastermind behind the bombing, not Dena. He also figured that Ahmed had followed you and him to San Francisco, had been there all along, not in San Diego as he had led you to believe. That's when Kasim figured that it was Ahmed who killed Slagg. He was about to call the police when Ahmed arrived at the motel in Avila Beach. Kasim confronted him, hoping to give you time to get to Dena's. He said he figured she'd convince you she was innocent and that Tafiq was really Ahmed and that he was dangerous."

Theo nodded. "Yeah, she tried. By the time I got it—it was almost too late—he found us."

Agent Aubrey continued. "Apparently. Tafiq figured that out, too. He shot Kasim and got Dena's address off his computer."

Theo fell back onto the pillows, clutching her stomach.

Abby, who was studying her, moved closer to the bed. "Hey, you okay?"

"It's just that . . . ."

"You gonna be sick?"

Theo took some deep breaths and let them out slowly. When the icy clenching in her gut abated, she said, "I'm okay. It's just that I keep feeling that hit. It's the shock of it."

She looked at Abby. "I just can't shake it."

Abby took Theo's free hand gently in her own. "You will, Theo. You will. This will all become a distant memory. Right now, though, you need to rest and recover."

Abby nodded to Agent Aubrey, "You think we can give this a rest for right now?"

"Absolutely," Aubrey said. "Here's my card. Call me if you need to. Either of you."

Aubrey was turning to leave when Theo said, "Is Kasim going to be okay?"

"Absolutely. He came through surgery and is doing fine last I knew. You can call him at the hospital. Oh, and just so you know, the SFPD aren't pressing charges for impersonating an officer. They just want the name and location of the counterfeiter who made up the fake badges and ID."

Theo looked blank. "Oh, yeah. I'm sure Kasim will cooperate," she said, seriously doubting that he would.

Agent Aubrey jotted a phone number down on a slip of paper and laid it on the table tray. "I'm sure he'd like to hear from you, Theo. Your name was the only thing the EMTs could get out of him when they got to the motel. Last I knew he was still worried about you."

Theo smiled—glowed, actually. Learning that Kasim had survived and that he wasn't part of Ibrahim's cover-up was good news. "I will. I'll call him right now! Thank you, Agent—," she paused. "Is Aubrey your first or last name?"

"Last. My first name is Daniel."

"Thank you, Daniel."

Abby picked up the phone and placed the call. Kasim picked up almost immediately.

"Mr. Jabul, this is Abby Archer. I'm a friend of Theo's. She'd like to talk to you."

26

"Theo?"

"Kasim! I'm so happy to hear your voice."

"Yeah. Me, too. Wasn't sure I'd be hearing much of anything after Ibrahim shot me." Kasim added with a chuckle, "Good thing he was a lousy shot."

Theo's gut clenched. The thought of metal ripping into flesh flashed in her head. She flinched. Her chest tightened. She couldn't speak.

"So how are you," Kasim was saying.

When she didn't immediately respond, he said, "Theo?"

The wave of nausea subsided enough for her to answer, "I'm . . . I'm fine. And you?"

"Hey, I'm good. I'm leaving here tomorrow—leastwise that's the doc's promise."

Theo nodded. "Glad to hear it.

"How's Dena? She okay?

"I haven't seen her yet. But her husband and kids came to see me. They said she's going to be okay. Looks like we all are."

"How's your arm?" he asked.

"I don't know really. It's bandaged up. I'll know more when those come off. How about you?"

"A couple of broken ribs. I think he was aiming for my heart. It only hurts when I laugh," he said, adding an almost chuckle that sounded like a painful gasp.

Theo smiled. "So, you get out tomorrow?"

"They're talking tomorrow. You know how that goes. Maybe the next day. I'd prefer today. Apparently, what I want doesn't matter."

Theo paused, then said, "When did you know?"

"After you left for Dena's," he said. "Something—lots of somethings—didn't add up. I started playing back our steps. When Slagg was killed, I was certain we were being followed. It never occurred to me it was him, though." He paused. "I should have seen it, Theo. I missed too many clues."

"Don't," she said. "Don't beat yourself up over this, Kasim. You trusted him. Why wouldn't you. He had been your mentor. No one would have thought he had any other motive other than to reunite me with my mother and to discover if his brother had a child. Just another one of his lies."

Kasim was silent for a moment, then, "I don't think he lied about that, Theo. I think he did love your mother. Scientists say there's a fine line between loving and hating. It's the passion circuits—they're identical in structure."

"That's a terrifying thought!"

"Yeah. Probably best to not think about that one," he said.

"Here's what I can't seem to grasp," she said. "Why kill innocent people? He didn't even hit his target which was O'Keefe. And he knew that. So why do it. To make a point?"

"Several years before he went after O'Keefe, his brother, the real "Tafiq," was killed in Paris by the Mossad who were targeting high-ranking officials of the PLO. His brother was nothing more than 'collateral damage'—that's how they saw it. Ahmed never forgot that—and he couldn't forgive."

"Did he say why he was willing to kill Dena—if he ever loved her at all?"

"No. He didn't discuss that with me. He simply said he had a bigger mission now. He said he couldn't let anything interfere with that. Not Dena. Not you. And not me. Then he shot me."

Theo felt a sudden chill. "I'm sorry, Kasim," she said. "I'm sure you were close."

Kasim didn't respond to that. After a pause he asked, "How're you connecting with Dena?"

Theo hesitated. "Good—rather—okay, I guess. I haven't seen her yet."

"And her family's there, for both of you, sounds like."

"Yeah."

"You having some trouble with that, Theo?"

She sighed. "Yeah. A little."

"Baby steps, Theo. That's all. Baby steps."

She nodded. "Good advice, as always."

"Theo, did Dena tell you if she had Ahmed's child or not?

Theo hesitated, unsure about what to say or if Dena had told her family the truth yet.

"I don't know. We didn't have time to clear that up."

Theo heard other voices on Kasim's end.

"My doctor just showed up, Theo. Can I call you later?"

"Please. You know where I am and how to reach me?"

"Yeah. I have my computer," he said, laughing.

27

Physical scar-tissue heals—eventually. Mental scars can run deeper and take years to heal. Some never do.

Theo tossed the letter onto the pile on the kitchen counter. It was the third one she'd received in as many weeks. All were from Dena. She hadn't opened any of them.

She busied herself: poured kibbles into KC's bowl, rearranged her rack of Keurig K-cups—decaf on top, French roast below; wiped down the counter, tossed the towel in the dirty clothes basket on top of the washer in the laundry room. Then she selected a fresh dishtowel, rearranging the drawer in the process. Busy work. The perfect foil for not dealing with the issues piling up in her head.

The knock at the door didn't startle her. She knew it was Abby.

"It's open."

"Hey," Abby said, poking her head in. "Want some company?"

"Sure."

Abby scanned the kitchen and noted the neatly arranged counters.

"So, where is he?"

"What? Who?" Theo said. She was organizing the ceramic coffee cups in the cupboard by size, lining up the handles at perfect right-angles.

"The OCD alien who moved in and took over your body."

Abby leaned against the counter staring at the cupboard. "You auditioning for a photoshoot in *Home Beautiful* or are the Rockettes in town and popping in for coffee?

"I'm not obsessive-compulsive, Abs. It's just that I'm bored, I guess. Sam has me on forced R&R and I'm running out of things to do."

Abby eyed the pile of envelopes with Dena Seeger's return address. She picked them up.

"You planning to open these anytime soon?"

Theo reached over and grabbed them, flinging them back onto the counter.

"Sure. One of these days."

Abby raised an eyebrow. She changed the subject.

"Hey, how 'bout a walk down to Bailey's? I need to check on the place. I haven't really put in serious time since I've been nursing you back to health."

"I don't need a nursemaid!" she snapped. "You can stop checking up on me—I'm fine!"

Abby didn't budge. She folded her arms and leaned against the counter. "I can see that. You're in fine fettle—and sweet as a kitten."

"Don't patronize me, Abs. I'm in no mood for it."

"Clearly. You don't seem to need a thing." Abby headed for the door. "Well, see 'ya."

Theo slid into her desk chair and woke her computer from sleep.

"Bye," she said as the door closed on Abby's way out.

Her phone rang. She recognized the area code. It was Dena. She let it go to voice mail. A few moments later there was a knock at the door.

"It's open," she yelled.

Another knock.

Theo jumped up, irritated. She wrenched it open. "For Pete's sake, Abby, when did you ever bother to knock—"

"Hi, Theo," Dena said. "I figured I owed you an explanation. May I come in?"

Theo turned around and walked away, leaving the door ajar. "Whatever."

Dena closed the door quietly and took in the tiny living room. "This sure brings back memories. You've updated the furnishings, but it still has your grandmother's charm."

Theo headed into the kitchen. "Want some coffee or tea?"

"No thanks, honey. I don't want to put this off—while I still have the nerve."

"Coming here—I'd say you had plenty of nerve."

Dena glanced at the counter and saw her unopened letters. "Oh, Theo, do you hate me that much?"

"I don't hate you. I don't love you. I don't want anything to do with you."

Dena sank into the big club chair. She leaned back and closed her eyes.

Theo felt a pang of remorse. "Okay, that was harsh. I don't want to hurt you. I just can't bring myself to know what to do with you. You've been MIA in my life—all my life—and I managed to fill up all the space for my feelings about family with grandmother and my friends and … for Frank … whom I'll probably never see again. You see, Dena, there's just no room for any more … feelings … not for you … not for my brother and sister … not for anyone."

Dena looked down at her hands spread out on her knees.

"And," Theo narrowed her eyes. "By the way, did you tell Tom, Jr. who his father really is—*was*? Are you just going to add that to your arsenal of little lies?"

"Could I have some water?"

Theo grabbed a glass from the cupboard, filled it with chilled water and handed it to her.

Dena took a few sips and started to set it down. "Do you have a coaster?"

"Seriously? A coaster? That's all you've got? Your life is full of secrets and lies and you're worried about finding a damn coaster!"

Dena set the glass down. She hesitated, then cleared her throat, "I can't expect you to understand, Theo. To you, morality is black or white. Do you even know anything about the great grey abyss out there? You've lived long enough to know that some things are not that simple—life is not that simple."

"That's your explanation. That's your excuse. I don't get the moral concept of black-versus-white-versus-grey—that's all you have? There's the whole issue of falling for a terrorist! What the hell were you thinking?"

"Oh, Theo," Dena said, pressing her hand to her forehead. "I had hoped you'd understand—or at least would let me try to explain. You are hurt. I get that. But I never would have stayed away from you if I thought it was safe to connect with you. Ahmed was always in the back of my mind. I knew that if he thought I was still alive, he'd look for me and that would lead him to you.

"Fortunately, he was so busy trying to cover up his tracks and creating a new identity that he just took the police report as gospel. He wanted to believe I died in that bombing. It gave him a clean slate. He started over. Then, when he saw you at the university, he knew instantly who you were."

"Clever! Bring it back to me and the university. I suppose this is all my fault."

"No. None of this is your fault. You were—"

"Yeah, I know. Ahmed said it best: *collateral damage*."

Dena stood up and walked into the kitchen. She looked out the window. "Unit 3 was ours, your dad's and mine. That's where we lived for a few months until he was called up. We were happy here, Theo. He was so excited when I told him I was pregnant. We had so many plans …"

She turned around and faced Theo. "He was sure you were a boy. He wanted to name you after his favorite president—Theodore Roosevelt. I told him you might be a girl. He said, 'well, if *he* is a *she*, then name her Theodosia—she'll have guts and stamina and morals.' Looks like he was right."

"Thanks for the great name," she snapped. "I've had to explain it all my life."

Dena ignored the jab. "Did you know it means 'God's gift'?"

"Great! Okay, enough reminiscing. Let's talk about the real reason you're here. So, why *are* you here, Dena?"

"I want—*need*—to have you in my life—in your brother and sister's lives. Tom wants you to be part of the family. We all do. We've been separated too long."

"Uh huh. After all these years, your *needs* are the only thing that matters? The rest of us just have to get submissively on that train and ride into the sunset? I'd like to know what your husband and kids really think about all this?

"So. It bears repeating. Have you told my *brother* who his father really is?"

"No. And I don't intend to. I discussed it with Tom. He feels, as do I, that it would just hurt and confuse Tom Jr."

Theo nodded. "Sure. More lies. Why not. It's what you do best."

"Theo, sometimes the truth is too hurtful. What would Tom Jr. gain from knowing that?"

Theo walked over to the counter that separated the kitchen from the living room. She stood there staring at Dena in disbelief. "A lie is better than the truth? Is that what you just said?"

A tiny vein twitched in Dena's left temple. One side of her mouth turned up in a painful, almost smile. "Yes. Yes, sometimes a lie is kinder than the truth. Perhaps, someday Theo, you'll get that."

"I knew it," Theo said. "I knew you wouldn't be honest with him anymore than you've been honest with me. That's why I can't be part of your family. I'll always know the truth. And I'll always know that he *doesn't* know. And, right there, Dena, is where I draw the line. Lies—even little ones—even if they're just off the mark of the truth—lead to more lies. I've seen it before. I walked in that murky grey area between a falsehood and the facts. I've seen them ruin lives. I've been there when not telling the truth led to a cover-up and that led to someone's murder.

"What I know is this: lies—white, black, or murky grey—are always fatal. If they don't kill you for real, they kill the most precious thing that exists between humans—they kill the *trust*. You, of all people, Dena, should get that.

"Your son—my brother—deserves the truth. You owe it to him. He has the right to know who is father was. Your mistake shouldn't be his burden to bear, whether he's aware of it or not.

"Shouldn't he know about his family heritage, his roots, his ancestors? You don't own the patent on his personal heritage. It owns itself. And that's what belongs to him. You shouldn't deny him that."

"Theo, please. Please don't do this. After all these years I just want to have my family back together. We all want this. We want you to be part of our lives."

Theo walked over to the door and held it open.

"You should go. You can tell them I'm swamped with work right now. You can make up a story that I'll try to visit during the holidays. You're good at that—making up stories."

Dena stood at the doorway looking out into the patio. When she turned, tears glistened on her cheeks.

"My door is always open to you, Theo. I love you. I always will."

28

San Diego's fall came and went. A few days before Thanksgiving, Theo was shopping with Abby for green-bean casserole fixings—their contribution to the big Thanksgiving feast that Guy and Oren were hosting at *Las Casitas*.

Theo's arm was practically back to normal after a couple of months of physical therapy. Even her attitude was better.

"How many are we preparing for?" Theo asked while juggling two large cans of mushroom soup and a giant one of French-fried onion rings.

Abby was busy weeding through a huge pile of fresh green beans and stuffing handfuls into a plastic bag. "Besides tenants and guests—ten or twelve of us—I think Oren asked a couple stagehands and actors from the Old Globe who couldn't be with their families. We should make enough casserole for twelve."

On their way to the checkout, Abby stopped at the fresh-flower centerpieces and selected a beautiful arrangement with mini-pumpkins and red and gold azaleas in a ceramic orange pumpkin.

"Isn't this just too cute!"

Theo nodded approval and the deal was done.

When they got back to Theo's, there was a package sitting on the front porch.

"You order something from Amazon?"

Theo shook her head "no" and examined the label. It's from Harry and David.

"Harry and David who?" Abby asked.

"Not 'who'—what—it's a mail-order house. It's probably for one of my tenants. Maybe FedEx left it on my doorstep because they weren't home."

They took the package in and set it on the table while packing the fridge with their perishable groceries. That done, Abby checked the label.

"Says it's for 'Theo Hunter'—that would be you."

"Huh," Theo shrugged. "You open it."

Abby grabbed a knife and slit the sealing tape, revealing an inner box. She lifted it out and set it on the counter. "It's yours. You should open it."

Theo looked at it curiously, then popped the lid. Inside was a beautiful array of golden pears and apples, fresh cheeses, and bags of mixed nuts.

"Wow! This is super!" Abby said with glee. "Who's it from?"

Theo opened the gift envelope. "Happy Thanksgiving, Theo. From: Dena, the Two Toms and Abigail."

"Well," Abby said. "Isn't that nice."

"Yeah. Super," Theo said, tossing the card on the counter. "You can have it."

Theo walked away, disappearing into her bedroom.

"As much as I want to take you up on the offer," Abby shouted after her, "I think you should keep it." She walked to the bedroom and stood at the door. "I can always visit, you know."

Theo was standing at the bedroom window.

"You take it, Abs. I don't want it. I don't want it here."

"Even with every taste bud in my mouth salivating, I'm going to pass. I hate to be the victor who gets the spoils—especially in this tug-of-war between you and your mother."

"Abby, don't start."

Abby turned and headed into the kitchen. She shouted over her shoulder, "I could use a drink. How 'bout you?"

Theo followed her. "It's not even noon."

"It's five o'clock in Rio de Janeiro. And in the land of *Carni-val-e*—I'm pretty sure it's happy hour," Abby said, and poured Jack Daniels over ice in two glasses.

Theo took hers. Sipped it, then downed it. She turned to Abby. "Okay, so you want to talk, right?"

Abby paused with her glass to her lips. "Sure. Want another?"

Theo frowned. "Don't be ridiculous. It's just time to get this over and done with. I don't want to discuss it anymore."

"Okay. You start."

"I don't want to act as though I'm part of that family. I don't feel a connection. I won't live a lie. There. That's it. Satisfied?"

Abby set her drink on the counter. "What's really going on, Theo?"

"I told you."

"No. You just gave me a reason to cover up the real reason. That's not the truth."

"I can't tell you everything, Abby. My mother—and I use the word metaphorically—has a secret, something she needs to reveal. She won't. I called her on it and she still won't budge. That's it. Until she does the right thing, I refuse to be part of the lie."

"So, this secret is hers alone?"

"Yes and no."

"It affects someone else?"

"Yes."

"You?"

"I'm not saying anything further. I've said more than I want to. That's it. End of session."

Abby let it go.

Thanksgiving Day was dry and sunny, with a mild Santa Ana to thank for the warm fall day. Oren and Guy had set up three, six-foot tables with chairs in the patio. Abby and Theo decorated with white linen tablecloths, napkins, and china in several different patterns donated by tenants. Abby decided that one flowery centerpiece wouldn't do. She found two more so that each table had its own. The smells of roasting turkey, bread stuffing, mashed potatoes and gravy soon wafted out of several cottages as all the tenants shared the chore of baking, boiling, broiling, sautéing or frying any and every possible delectable item on Guy's menu.

At three o-clock sharp, casserole dishes appeared, candles were lit, and a happy chorus of laughter and banter filled the outdoor dining "room." When all were seated, Oren appeared with the guest of honor—a perfectly browned Tom Turkey on a platter rimmed with sliced cooked green applies, sage leaves, and purple grapes. Applause rippled and everyone lifted their flutes of champagne and toasted Guy and "Tom Turkey."

After every casserole dish had been passed at least twice, Oren stood up and made a toast. "I know we all have something to be thankful for. I think we should share that. Perhaps it's my overgenerous nature—or maybe it's just my third glass of this marvelous bubbly."

There were shouts of "hear, hear!" followed by, "It's the bubbly, Oren!" and lots of laughter.

Oren continued. "I'll start it off. I'm grateful for my life in sunny San Diego, for my wonderful Guy, and for all of you who make my world special. Thank you!"

There was applause and the sound of knives clinking lightly on the crystal glasses. Each, in turn, stood and made a toast. When it was Theo's turn, she thanked Oren and Guy for orchestrating a great Thanksgiving dinner and told her tenants and friends that she couldn't ask for a better group to share this special holiday with. She was still speaking when a collective gasp rose up from the assembled guests. Theo realized that all eyes that had been turned on her were now staring at something behind her. She turned.

A man stood at the end of the patio. Although he was much thinner than she remembered, Theo knew him instantly. It was Frank.

In a blur, Theo rushed to him and threw her arms around him. Suddenly, applause broke out and everyone left their places at the table to surround the couple.

"I thought … I was afraid you were …."

"I know. I'm sorry. I couldn't contact you—or anyone," he said. "But I'm done with that … and I'm here … and … I'm starving!"

Frank was ushered to a seat next to Theo and the food passing started all over again. More champagne appeared and Oren pulled out his guitar and began strumming the notes to Led Zeppelin's "Stairway to Heaven" … "There's a lady who's sure all that glitters is gold and she's buying a stairway to heaven …." rang out clear, if a little slurred.

The party didn't break up until after 10 p.m. Everyone shooed Frank and Theo off amid Theo's protesting that she needed to help clean up.

"I'll pack up some turkey and trimmings and slip them into your fridge," Abby said. "Don't worry about any of this. You two have a lot of catching up to do."

Oren piped up, "So that's what they call it!"

Frank and Theo didn't need a second invitation to disappear. They were off to Theo's bungalow while the crowd was still laughing and singing.

Sometime around 3 a.m., Theo woke up. Frank's arms encircled her. When she started to move, he grasped her tighter in his sleep. Then he woke up.

"Sorry, honey, I just … I just …"

"It's okay, Frank. I can't believe it either. I'm afraid I'll wake up and this will all be a dream."

He slipped his thumb over her lips and kissed her tenderly, then with more urgency. Soon they were melded together, moving in an intimate embrace, each clinging to the other as if they were afraid that this might end, but hoping that it wasn't fate's tease—trusting that tomorrow would come and that it had their names written all over it.

After, Frank held on to her. Theo felt his breath struggling. She pulled back and realized he was crying. His chest heaving in painful sobs.

"Frank, I'm right here. I'm not going anyplace."

He didn't speak for a few moments, then he said, "I thought I'd never see you again. The only thing that gave me hope was that I had to get back to you, Theo. That's what got me through it."

"We don't have to talk about what you went through," she said. "You can tell me in your own good time—or not. It's up to you. But I will be right here—I'm not going anywhere. I love you and, like some wise-guy once said, 'I don't think we'd be right for anyone else.'"

He chuckled. "I did say that, didn't I."

"Yeah," she whispered, nuzzling his ear. "And you are unanimous in that!"

It was after dawn when they stirred. They were both starving. Theo made them turkey sandwiches, which they washed down with hot coffee and pumpkin pie. Then they returned to bed and stayed there, not exactly sleeping, until noon.

"Wanna get up?" Theo asked.

"What for? I've got all I need right here," he said, snuggling and growling, nuzzling her neck.

Finally, at 3 p.m., they both decided they were hungry—again.

"More turkey?" Theo asked.

"I need a steak," Frank said. "Let's shower and head over to Island Prime on Harbor Island. I could eat a porterhouse—Kansas City style!"

So that's what they did.

29

The table was in a perfect glass corner of the steak house which was situated on pilings jutting out into the bay. Behind them, the city's skyline reflected onto the still water and shimmered along the harbor, postcard perfect.

They were savoring their Merlot. Frank polished off his porterhouse and was eyeing the remnants of Theo's filet which she kept pushing around the plate as if she'd grown bored with its perfect medium-rare succulence.

"You gonna eat that?"

"Guess I wasn't as hungry as I thought," she said, offering her plate to him.

"You don't have to ask me twice!"

The waiter swooped down on them the moment the last morsel disappeared.

"Would you like to see the dessert menu? An apéritif, perhaps?"

Theo asked for coffee. Frank did the same. "And the check, please."

Theo studied the milk swirling in her cup, trying to find the right words to start the inevitable conversation that needed vetting, the one that always ended in both of them agreeing to disagree.

"Frank …"

He reached across the table and cupped her hand in his and squeezed it. "Don't, Theo. I know what you're going to say."

"Do you? Do you know what it was like to think you were dead? We all did. Even Alex—even with pep talks: 'Frank is good at his job,' 'he's just deep undercover,' 'Frank knows what he's doing'—I heard them all. Not very convincing when I don't hear from you for months."

She pulled her hand away. It was trembling. "I thought … I thought you were dead!"

"Honey, please."

"Please? Please what? Please don't worry? Please trust me? Please … oh, I don't know…"

She fished around in her purse for a Kleenex, found one and blew her nose. "Look at that! You've got me whining and crying. I hate this!"

Frank leaned back in his chair and waited. Theo stopped fiddling with the Kleenex and looked up at him.

"Is that a smirk? Tell me that's not a smirk, Frank Marino! You think this is funny?"

"Not funny and I'm not laughing. It's just a little odd coming from someone who spent over a week in an L.A. hospital, recovering from a gunshot wound—which was just a hair from being fatal."

"That wasn't how it was supposed to end. I had no idea what was going on when I—"

"When you met some shady character at night in the church parking lot, then took off to San Francisco with a computer hacker to find your mother—a suspected terrorist?

"You're a fine one to point the finger, Miss Investigative Reporter."

"Okay. I'll admit that, in retrospect—"

"*In Retrospect.* Seriously, Theo? You should have called the FBI the moment you opened that envelope and found the locket. What were you thinking?"

"In my defense, I didn't think it was all that dangerous—at first."

"The operative word here is *think!* You took a chance. You nearly didn't survive this one. And it wasn't even part of your job!"

"Oh, and it's okay because your near-death experience was? What a crock!"

"Theo, stop. Listen to me for one minute."

She let out a big sigh and folded her arms. "Sure."

"This assignment saved lives. Young girls and boys were rescued from a life of slavery—sex trafficking. Some were as young as 12, Theo. Just kids. Yes. It was dangerous. But I had an amazing crew working with me. We did the impossible—the unthinkable—we beat the gangs, the cartel, the perverts. We got them and we got those kids away from them."

"Yes, Frank. I'm proud of you for that. I'm grateful and I'm happy for those you saved. But, how many on your team were lost?"

"One," he said, looking away. "I lost one."

"I'm sorry. I can understand how your team is your family and how hard it is to suffer any loss."

Frank was studying the city skyline. Theo could see the muscles in his jaw flexing. It was obvious that Frank was still working through that loss. Theo knew that those were the kind of scars that would take a long time to heal—if ever.

The waiter offered coffee refills.

Theo cleared her throat. "So … where do we go from here?"

"I don't understand," Frank said. "What do you mean? I thought it was obvious. We love each other. We take the next step."

"Yes. It's what we both want. But what happens when you take on another assignment? What if you disappear again—for months—and no one knows where you are. What am I supposed to think? That this time, *you're* the one that got *lost*? What then?"

Her eyes glistened and her voice cracked. "Tell me, Frank. What do I do—*then?*"

Frank rose. "C'mon, let's get outta here."

Outside, the wind had picked up and the temperature dropped. Theo shivered. Frank slipped his sports coat around her shoulders. "Let's walk along the docks."

They walked a short distance before both decided it was too chilly. They headed for Frank's car.

The drive back to Theo's was quiet. KC met them at the door, complaining about his empty food bowl. Theo went through the feeding routine silently. Frank disappeared into the bedroom.

If KC noticed the chill in the room he ignored it. The moist salmon pâté had his full attention. Frank shed his shoes and slipped into the sweats that he kept at Theo's. Theo headed to the bathroom, taking longer than usual to wash up for bed. When he heard the shower running, Frank poured himself a double Jack Daniels over ice and settled into the big club chair.

About thirty minutes later, Theo appeared, wet hair pulled back, face scrubbed, sweats and floppy slippers—an ensemble that telegraphed a very clear message—the opposite of one conveyed by a sexy negligee.

"Can I fix you a nightcap?" Frank said, trying to sound cheerful.

"I'm good."

"Theo, we …," he didn't get to finish.

"What?" she snapped. "What's to say? It's status quo—right? Business as usual."

"Theo, that's not fair."

"No. It's not. But it's how I feel."

She picked up the remote and switched on the news station.

Presently, Frank said, "Well, I'm heading to bed."

"Okay. I'll be there in a little bit."

That night, Theo slept on the couch. She awoke to the smell of fresh coffee. Frank was in the chair reading the paper.

"Morning," he said cheerily.

"Hi," Theo mumbled, trying to focus bleary eyes. Guess I conked out. Sleep okay?"

"I've slept better…with you," Frank said.

Theo brewed a cup of coffee and returned to the couch, grabbing the local section of the paper.

Frank's cell phone buzzed.

"Yeah. Uh-huh. Sure. About twenty minutes. Okay."

"Theo, I have to go to the local bureau office for a couple of hours. Wanna do lunch?"

"Sure. Just let me know if you decide to take another six-month assignment. I might want to eat before next May."

Frank ignored her, got dressed and headed for the door. "Be back around noon. Be here. Please."

Then he was gone.

She tossed the paper at the door.

30

At 11:55 a.m., sharp, Frank returned. Theo was still in her sweats.

"I thought you'd be dressed."

Theo had been rehearsing her speech. By now, she was fuming.

"I wasn't sure you'd be back."

He crossed the distance from the door to the couch in three strides. He pulled her up into his arms and kissed her square on the mouth, ignoring her squirming. When he finished, he tossed her back onto the couch.

"What the hell was that!" she flared up at him. You think that solves everything, don't you? A little kiss, a big hug, a roll-around beneath the sheets—then everything is just fine! That's what you think? It's not, Frank. It's not fine!"

Frank walked away. Theo followed him. "Don't you walk away from me, Frank. This isn't over! I've not even begun!"

Frank slipped off his jacket, undid his tie, his shirt, and tossed them in a chair. When he reached for his belt, Theo crossed her arms.

"Don't."

"Don't what? Do this?"

He undid his belt.

"I mean it, Frank, we're not jumping into bed to solve this."

He kicked off his shoes, then unzipped his pants. He let them drop to the floor.

Her eyes flared. "Are you listening to me?"

When he slipped his thumbs into the waistband of his shorts, she shrieked, "Okay. Stop! Stop it!"

He did. Then he slid down onto the bed, fluffed up the pillows and patted the sheets. "Come here, Theo."

She crossed her arms and shook her head "no."

"Come on," he whispered. "We need to talk."

"That's what you mean by talk—you're such a typical male … "

"Come here, honey," he crooned again. "Please."

She glared at him. "I'll sit here on the side of the bed and we can talk. No touching!"

Frank leaned back into the pillows.

"What's it gonna take?" he said quietly. "What is it you really want?"

"I want … "she looked away. "I want you not to go off on those horrible assignments. I want you whole—here. Not gone, and not … dead!"

"Your wish is my command," he said, bowing.

"Don't joke. Frank I'm serious."

"Okay. Here's the latest. I was called into the office. The Washington bureau chief was in town. I met with him."

"Doesn't San Diego have a bureau chief?"

"Yes. Now," he said and smiled.

"What? What's that mean?"

"You, my dear, are looking at the new San Diego bureau chief."

For once, Theo was stunned. She stared. Then she found her voice and broke into a big smile. "You mean it! You're here—for good?"

"Yep. Well, for as long as I don't screw up!"

Theo cleared the distance between them in a single leap—right into his arms.

Frank rolled over and kissed her. "You know there's a ceremony that goes with this honor."

"Oh, Frank. Of course, there would be. When is it? Can I be there?"

He slipped her sweatshirt over her head and helped her wriggle out of the bottoms. "Actually, you are—here—I mean." He rolled over on his back and pulled her on top of him. She leaned in and kissed him. Then she raised up, looking skeptical.

"No more long undercover assignments?"

"That's right. Now, I'm the bastard that does the assigning."

Theo smiled. Then she laughed. Then she leaned in and whispered into his ear, "I can't believe this. It's a wish come true."

Frank slipped his hands down her back, pressing her against him. "I guess you could say I found the magic lamp and got my wish."

"I hear you get two more wishes," she whispered. "Know what else you want?"

Frank didn't answer, he rolled over on one elbow. Theo slipped under him and noticed he'd managed to lose his shorts in the process.

"You can have all my wishes… you just have to rub my magic lamp."

They both broke up laughing. Then, she did just that.

31

"Don't you think that's a little premature?" Theo said. "We haven't set a date and I really, really, don't want a big fuss."

Abby and Oren were sitting at the tiny dining room table, scouring *Bridal Bazaar* magazine and ripping out pages with photos of bridal gowns, flower arrangements, reception place settings, and guest favors.

"Don't be silly," Oren said. "This is a once-in-a-lifetime event—or should be—you want it to be perfect. It's our job to make it so."

Theo looked a little lost. She reached for the coffee to brew another cup, her third that morning, and watched the flurry of excitement at her dining room table with the silence of veiled panic.

"Ooooh," Oren gasped. "Let's do deep periwinkle for the bridesmaids!" He brandished a photograph of a model enshrouded in yards of trailing satin. The couture look was topped with a demure lacy fascinator, its veil pulled across her face and into a bow in back and nestled into a mound of soft blond curls.

"Naw," Abby scowled. "Too much satin and lace. You'd think *she* was the bride. We'd have to double the bride's train just to make a statement."

A headache exploded across Theo's forehead. She leaned into the sink and closed her eyes, hoping she would vomit. The patter continued until she cupped her hands over her ears.

"Stop it! Just … please, please stop this. We'll just elope."

Abby and Oren froze mid-ad clipping and stared at her.

Oren said, "You can't be serious!"

Abby chimed in. "Frank's a Catholic. His whole Italian clan are Catholics with roots back to Emperor Constantine no doubt. *You* used to be one. How can you even *think* of eloping?"

"Sweetie—you have no choice!" Oren added. "They're going to want a *huge* Italian wedding with all the trimming's—BIG church wedding—BIG reception—BIG Dance. All of it! It's an insult if you don't go along with it."

"I haven't even met them yet."

Abby stared. Her mouth dropped open. "What? You're kidding. Right?"

"No. I'm not kidding. I've never met his family. He is going to tell his mom, sisters and brother. Then I'm going to meet them."

Abby laughed scornfully. "Oh, no, honey. That's not how it's done. Tell her, Oren. Tell her what the three stages of marrying an Italian are."

Oren leaned back in the chair.

"Act 1: *The Set Up*: Frank invites you to Sunday dinner with the family. You make nice and act like one of the girls. You get invited back. You do this for a couple of months. You cozy up to his mother, his sisters, his brother's wife, maybe an aunt or two. You praise the food and ask for recipes, you offer to babysit a couple of times—this gets you in good with the gals and the rug-rats. You hang out; go shopping, have lunch out. You know, girl stuff. They get used to you and think it's normal for you to be hanging around.

"After you've buttered up the clan, you and Frank invite the family to dinner at a very nice restaurant. Could be an Italian restaurant in Little Italy. Either way, there should be wine—lots and lots of wine. After dinner, Frank makes his announcement: 'I've asked Theo to marry me and she's accepted.' He produces a little velvet box, pops the lid, flashes the big rock. Everyone gasps at the brilliance (and size). Then he slips that little hunk of paradise on your finger. You smile. Applause all around!

"Act 2: *The Cinch*: They call it this because everything gets out of control and that little noose tightened to the point where you feel like you're strangling in wedding plans and traditions, which, by the way, includes nine months counseling and preparation by the local priest at the Italian church. You haven't done it right until you've been counseled about the duties and responsibilities of a good Catholic family by a guy who probably isn't acquainted with sex or marriage—well, maybe sex—who knows. Then, the family tries to take over the wedding production. That's where Abby and I come in. We're *your* 'wedding consultants.' We put the restraints on. We run interference. We do it *our* way—not ruffling any feathers on either side, of course. *You* don't get blamed for anything. *Perfect!*

"Act 3: *The Big Day*: Finally, the big day arrives. You march down that aisle in triumph. You got your man, sweetie!

"*The end.*"

Theo blanched. "Frank didn't tell me any of this."

"Doubt if he knows. He's a guy," Oren said. "He's lived it all his life and so it doesn't seem foreign to him. He probably thinks it's no big deal."

She set her coffee cup down on the counter and walked out of the kitchen into the patio. She kept walking—for blocks. She tried to process what Abby and Oren were saying. By the time she stood at the intersection of University Avenue and Sixth Avenue—nearly ten blocks from home—she had made a decision. She turned around and headed back.

Oren and Abby were still making lists, organizing their clippings, and talking over the details of the big extravaganza. Theo walked in. They didn't even look up.

"Stop," she said quietly. "Stop this."

That's when they looked at her as if she'd just landed from Mars.

"Frank and I will be married—in church. Frank's family and my closest friends will be there. I'll wear a suit—not white—and so will Frank. After, we'll come back here and have a small reception in the patio. Oren, you handle that. Abby, you and I'll go shopping for my outfit. We'll meet with his family—my first time—and we'll announce that we're getting married. That's it. Done."

With that Theo walked past the two, through the bedroom, then into the bathroom and closed the door. She took a shower.

Abby and Oren stood in her wake, looking as if they'd just been doused with a firehose.

The kitchen door opened and Frank came in. "Hi, guys," he said cheerily, then saw their expressions. "What's wrong?"

They told him.

"I'll talk to her," he said and disappeared into the bedroom.

Abby and Oren jumped up from the table and dashed to the closed door, put their ears to wood, and listened.

"Can you hear anything," Abby whispered.

"The shower stopped." Oren said. "Now, I hear voices."

"What are they saying?"

He shook his head. "Can't tell."

Then, they both heard: "Let's tell them."

The two eavesdroppers made a dash back to the table just as the door opened and Theo and Frank walked into the room. Oren and Abby pretended busy work.

"It's settled," Frank said. "We'll do it Theo's way."

Abby let out a big sigh. "You do know that your family is going to want something very different. Something traditional."

"I do," he said. He looked at Theo and smiled. "That felt good!"

"It's a little premature," she said, laughing.

"Okay, what about an engagement party?" Oren said. "At least let us do that."

Frank looked at Theo. She shook her head "no."

"Nope. Just the small wedding with a reception here, in the patio. And that's final."

There was silence. Then, "Okay. If that's how you want it," Abby said. "When?"

"How about next week?"

"No fuss. No muss," Frank was grinning. "No endless weeks and months of planning. No worries!"

"I want Abby to be my witness," Theo said, smiling.

"My brother Dominic will be mine," added Frank.

"What if it rains?" piped up Oren.

"It won't," Theo and Frank said in unison, grinning at each other.

That night, Frank and Theo returned from the impromptu gathering of the Marino clan at his mother's house. It had gone surprisingly well. They had all known about Theo, just never met her. They sized her up and decided she was right for Frank. They shared celebratory wine. Frank told them the date and his mother choked.

"Frank! That's too soon. We can't make the arrangements at the church. What about the parties, the dresses, the flowers …?"

"We want it this way, Ma. Simple. Quiet. Just with the people who mean everything to us." He hugged her. She melted.

His eldest sister Nina piped up, "You can't get married in the church without going through Pre-Cana. No priest will marry you!"

"Have it covered. We talked to a family friend, Father Tony Machado. He's a decorated Navy chaplain, a Catholic priest in good standing. He'll do it."

Frank shot down every one of their concerns quicker than nailing the target at a shooting range.

"What about your family, Theo?" his mother, Maria, asked. "Will they be able to be here on such short notice?"

Theo didn't flinch. "Yes. My family will be here."

Heading back home, Frank was upbeat. "Well. That went well!"

"Uh-huh, except for the part where I lied to your mom about my *family*."

"You gonna call your mother?"

"If I do, they'll probably come."

"You should do it, Theo."

"I know."

That night she sent the email. In less than thirty minutes her phone rang.

"Theo, it's Dena."

"I know."

"Do you really want us to come to your wedding? We'd love to—but that's not the question. Do *you* want us there?"

"I don't want to lie to Frank's mom or his sisters and brother. I told them you would be here. They believe me."

"Then it's set," Dena said.

"What can we give you for a wedding present?"

"Nothing. Just show up."

32

December 21st, just a few days before Christmas, Theo and Frank stood at the altar at Our Lady of the Rosary Church in San Diego's Little Italy. Frank's family had swelled from his mother, brother and his wife and three kids, his sister, her husband and two kids, and his youngest sister, to an additional three aunts and uncles, and fifteen cousins and their spouses and/or girl- or boyfriends. Alex Thorkensen, Frank's old boss, and her husband, Charlie, rounded out Frank's side of the church.

Theo's side was smaller: Abby, Oren and Guy, and the other tenants at *Las Casitas*. Sam, her boss from *The Tattler* and his wife. Her mother, Dena, and step-father Tom, her sister Abigail, and her brother Tom Jr., all showed up as promised.

Father Anthony Machado, Theo's childhood friend and undisputed teen years heart-throb, officiated. After much prodding from Abby and Oren, Theo agreed to a classically elegant Adrianna Papell full-length gown, in soft dove-grey, featuring a shimmering, illusion bodice with Bateau neckline. The sleeves were short. She carried a single red rose.

Frank wore a blue suit with a rose boutonniere.

The ceremony was simple. Linda, the church organist, played the traditional songs. The exit march—a rousing rendition of Iron Butterfly's "In-A-Gadda-Da-Vida"—was a special request of the groom.

Dinner was moved from the *Las Casitas* garden due to a forecast of rain. Instead, Oren managed to pull more than a few strings and got a wedding dinner cruise aboard one of the *Hornblower* yachts. The champagne flowed, and the rain held off.

Frank and Theo did the obligatory dances with all the relatives and friends.

When it was his turn, Tom Jr. asked if she wouldn't mind just going for a walk. "I'm a lousy dancer," he said.

Theo agreed and was grateful for the break.

The ship was slowly taking a turn around the west end of the bay, skirting Point Loma. The old Cabrillo Lighthouse blinked high above the point. It was a beautiful night for a party.

A waiter passed and Tom snagged fresh champagne flutes. He handed one to Theo and raised his in a toast. "I hope you find all the happiness you deserve, Theo."

"Thanks, Tom. I'm not sure what that means—but if we can just have the rest of our lives together, that'll be all I need."

They leaned against the railing and looked out at the city lights in the distance. The silence became awkward, Theo spoke up.

"How's the internship going?"

"It's good. Long hours. But worth it."

"When did you know you wanted to be a doctor?"

"Always. It was because of dad. He's one of the best. Guess I just want to be like him."

Theo nodded. She took a sip of champagne and tried to come up with another topic that wasn't about the family dynamic and the approaching holidays—or about the other taboo issue: Tom and his *father*.

"So, with those 12-hour workdays, when do you have time for fun?"

Tom laughed. "Fun? What's that?"

Theo nodded, smiled, and looked around, hoping someone else would show up to rescue the conversation.

After a moment, he said, "We don't have to make small talk, Theo. Mom told me the truth about Ahmed. Who he was."

"A terrorist, you mean?"

"My father."

Theo nodded. "I see. And ..."

"And, I'm okay with it. I mean, I get it."

"Tom, you are your own person. You know that, right? What Ahmed was—what he did—isn't who you are. His life, his losses, those had an influence on him. I wouldn't say they made him what he was, but his culture, his beliefs, those form a strong bond. In some, they are enough to justify violence."

"You don't have to explain him to me, Theo. I get it. I'm not him. I'm me. He was smart. I have his DNA—along with my mom's. But who I am is the product of my parents, my mom and my dad. I have a different morality thanks to them. I think I can be a good doctor and, just maybe, a decent human being."

Theo nodded. "You already are." Then, she hugged him.

"Does Abigail know?"

"Yeah."

"And how's that going?"

"It's okay. I mean, Abbie always thought I was the product of alien spawn ..." He cast her a sideways glance and snickered.

Theo laughed out loud.

It might have been the heart-to-heart with Tom, or maybe it was the champagne, but Theo grabbed him and held him for a long moment. She was surprised to feel the dampness of tears on her cheeks.

"I'm not usually gushy! Probably the booze," she said, laughing.

"I hope we see more of you, Theo. Abbie and I want us to be … family."

Theo cleared her throat, surprised at the lump there. "My, er…, family skills are a work in progress. But I've been told I'm a fast learner," she said, wiping away more tears.

Tom raised his glass. "Here's to *la familia*, Theo. Long may we blaze!"

Theo and Tom Jr. were joined by Abigail who brought in reinforcements in the form of the waiter with more champagne. The conversation flowed almost as fast as the wine. They made some jokes and shared a little political and philosophical perspectives. They didn't agree on everything, but it was enough. They did agree to get together over the holidays to hash out the differences.

Abby found them, then Oren and Guy. Pretty soon there was a lot more laughter.

Frank showed up to spirit her away to a final turn around the dance floor as the ship was heading back to the dock.

Oren and Guy corralled them. Oren handed Frank an envelope. "We didn't know what to get you. We decided the Presidential Suite at the Courtyard Marriott downtown would be the perfect getaway for tonight. When we dock, say your good-byes, and climb into the limo waiting there. The rest of the evening belongs to just the two of you."

The view was breathtaking from the suite on the 14th floor. Up close, the San Diego skyline and the harbor glittered all around them. The suite was larger than Theo's cottage, 1,000 square feet of beautifully appointed Italian Romanesque Revivial-style luxury. The sitting room could easily host a wedding reception, and probably had. It was the perfect honeymoon suite.

"All that's missing is a 'magic fingers' bed." Frank joked, "and a roll of quarters."

"I'll bet you could get one if you dialed the concierge," Theo giggled.

Frank popped the cork on the champagne and poured two glasses. He nibbled on the charcuterie board laid with cheeses including aged Gouda and chunks of salty Parmigiano-Reggiano. There were several buttery varieties including Brillat-Savarin, and Theo's favorites were the crumbly Chèvre goat cheese and Gorgonzola. Frank's personal delights—the cured meats—were enough to fill the larder at an Italian deli. There was also plenty of crackers, crusty bread, crisp, cold grapes and a jar of honey to drizzle on every scrumptious bite.

Hard to believe that after the fabulous dinner aboard the *Hornblower* that they could be hungry; yet, they were starving! They dove into the array like the famished.

They were sitting on the floor, the double glass doors to the balcony were thrown wide open, while the two, still in their wedding finery, were busy savoring the last nibble of goodies. A feeling of supreme happiness washed over Theo. She turned to Frank. "It was the perfect wedding, wasn't it?"

Frank was busy licking honey from his fingers. "You liked it?"

"I loved it! It was *perfect!*" She purred. "Our friends, our families, and I say that plural—were all there. And, and, they *like* us—they really, really like us!"

Frank smiled.

"Go ahead, Frank. You think I'm drunk. But it couldn't have been better."

Frank topped off their glasses. "Make peace with your mother, did you?"

Theo smiled and nodded. "She told the truth, Frank. I didn't think she would. But she did."

"Your brother okay with that?"

"Yes. Yes, he is."

"Okay, then. So, here's a little truth I've been saving for this very moment. I love you. I think we're perfect for each other. I want to hug you to pieces and pour this honey all over you. Then, I'll lick it off. What do you think about that?"

Theo giggled—then hiccupped. "I think we're both plastered!"

"Yes. Yes, my dear. *That* is the *truth*!"

Theo snuggled up to Frank. They didn't even finish their champagne. Within minutes, there on the floor with the million-dollar view of San Diego's harbor spread out before them, and wrapped in each other's arms, they both fell fast asleep.

The End

Acknowledgements

Heartfelt thanks to my editor Dave Feldman.

The character Sam Morley, editor of *The Tattler*, is not exactly patterned after Dave—close, but not really. However, just as Sam pushes Theo to work beyond her comfort level, without Dave's support, nagging, and encouragement, *Fatal Little Lies* would still be sitting in my "to do" box.

After more than thirty years in the newspaper business, Dave, a keen storyteller himself, is finally working on his own memoir: *For Zee Whole Night? And Other Tales from a Newspaperman's Outrageously Rewarding Life.*

You owe it to yourself to take a peek into the real world of print news from the pen of a man with a keen eye for story.

Thank you, Dave. It's been a pleasure to learn from the true Renaissance Man of Letters.

Grateful appreciation to Barbara Crothers for her careful edits. Barbara is a poet and memoir chronicler whose fascinating real-life stories have been published in multiple editions of *The Guilded Pen* anthologies.

Many thanks to Mardie Schroeder for her support and careful final review. Mardie, president of the San Diego Writers and Editors Guild, divides her time between promoting local authors, and "acing" those opponents on the tennis court. Mardie's epic novel, *Go West for Luck, Go West for Love*, a multi-generational love story in a western setting, is in its second printing.

Finally, to David Wehlage for his accurate, detailed instructions and sage advice on navigating the streets of Los Angeles and the abandoned Los Angeles subway system. Dave is a renowned multiple Emmy and Golden

Mike award winning photo journalist and a son to make any mother proud. In this case, he's mine.

Author's Notes

Fatal Little Lies is a work of fiction. While the characters are figments of the author's imagination, they are modeled after composites of many types: those with inquisitive minds, seeking out mysteries and solving them; those who are haunted by their past and anxious to right the wrongs they may have committed; and those who only wish to obliterate their mistakes and anyone who might bear witness to them.

Images and descriptions of locations in San Diego, San Francisco, Avila Beach, and other locals in California's coastal region were used merely as props for the situations as they occur, and to support the action scenes. They do not depict or reflect any specific incidents nor do they refer to any actual person, living or dead.

Fatal Little Lies is the third in the Theo Hunter Mystery Series and follows *Dirty Little Murders* and *Deadly Little Secrets*.

Theo Hunter's character was first introduced in *Dirty Little Murders* when her life was at its worst.

As an investigative reporter for San Diego's major newspaper, her job was to uncover the city's dirty secrets lurking behind a tourist Mecca image. But exposing a devious political takeover made her a casualty of vicious politics.

Fired from her job, her reputation shot, and deserted by the man she loved, Theo didn't think her life could sink any lower. But when the grisly discovery of a friend's battered body becomes a police cover-up led by her ex-fiancé, Theo vows to discover the truth. Soon she is on a collision course with dangerous forces.

Her meddling exposes a political scandal that threatens to topple the city's powerful kingpins. Uncovering corruption at the highest level of government comes with a price. Unprotected and on her own, Theo becomes the target of a ruthless killer.

> "A mystery/thriller . . . political misdeed with a tilt toward crime noir … believable!"
> — **Kirkus Reviews**

Deadly Little Secrets — When the slaying of a retired priest is shrouded in secrets, lies and cover-up, Theo is catapulted right into the middle of it. It all starts when an old flame, now a U.S. Navy chaplain and a priest, asks her to find out if the murdered priest was the innocent victim of a deranged killer—or a pervert who deserved what he got. Theo is hell-bent to find out.

But when her prime suspects are murdered, only one fact is clear … the killer will strike again. Armed with nothing but a madman's cryptic notes, Theo scrambles to decipher the clues while the killer lurks in the shadows, poised to silence her for good.

2015 Finalist—Best Mystery Category – **San Diego Book Awards**

Intriguing mystery with a full-bodied cast of characters. Abby and Theo have a good rapport … Very Thin Man. **—Writers Digest**

"Highly recommended good read."
San Diego Writers/Editors Guild

About the Author

Loren Zahn is the pseudonym of **M. Lee Buompensiero**, author of the highly acclaimed and award-winning novel, *Sumerland*, a tale of betrayal and deliverance.

Set in San Diego, and spanning three generations of a family's history, Buompensiero's work was inspired by a true story—hers!

Buompensiero's own grandparents were living in San Diego, California in 1926 when her grandfather lost his job at the Naval Air Station based in Coronado. He was offered work at a steel mill in his home town, Pittsburgh, Pennsylvania. Buompensiero's grandmother, recovering from tuberculosis, was unable to travel and remained in San Diego with their eldest son. Her grandfather and the two youngest children (a girl and a boy) journeyed to Pittsburgh. For whatever reason, the grandparents never reunited—the children had no contact with one another throughout their lives. Each married and had children of their own. Whether through design or as a result of the grandparents' estrangement and stubbornness, the siblings never reunited throughout the ensuing decades. All communication between the two sides of the family was lost, leaving no trail for the descendants to follow.

The family's reuniting, nearly 90 years later, is attributed to clever sleuthing by great-granddaughter Lynn and, very possibly, the intervention of the long, dead, dearly departed grandparents.

In her own words Buompensiero says: "*Sumerland* is told as a ghost story, inspired by my own family history. While we cannot prove that ghostly intercession by our long-dead grandparents helped bring the family together, we'd like to think that our reuniting was due to their efforts. Perhaps the dearly departed do get another chance to set the record straight and fix their mistakes—even after they are gone. We'd like to think so."

Buompensiero also penned the Theo Hunter Mysteries inspired by the deep, dark secrets, cover-ups and unsolved crimes of her native city, San Diego.

When not researching her next mystery novel, Buompensiero promotes the local writing arts as managing editor of *The Guilded Pen* anthologies, an annual publication of the San Diego Writers and Editors Guild. She is also a member of the national organization Sisters in Crime and its affiliate, Partners in Crime.

Sumerland

M. Lee Buompensiero

Francis and Marie-Claire Liebersohn have unfinished business. They want someone to set the record straight—seventy years after their deaths.

Kate Post just inherited the old Liebersohn mansion—her estranged mother's bizarre bequest to the daughter she rarely saw and barely knew. Kate doesn't want the house, but an odd inscription etched in concrete beside a garden pathway haunts her dreams, driving her back to the old place.

Sumerland (cont'd)

Convinced that a period restoration will make for a quick sale, she begins renovating. But Kate's plans and the Liebersohns' scheme are about to collide. The result will unhinge Kate's world, uncover haunting family secrets, and set her on a mission to undo the wrongs that only she can set aright.

2017 WINNER – Best Mystery Category

San Diego Book Awards

A lyrical harmony of mystery, romance, and the webwork of family. Buompensiero's Sumerland is a true page turner . . . so deeply human and lovingly written.

—Richard Lederer
Columnist, "San Diego Union Tribune"
and bestselling author of *Anguished English*

Vist us at:

http://www.greycastlepublishing.com

Theo Hunter Mysteries: *Dirty Little Murders*, *Deadly Little Secrets*, and *Fatal Little Lies*, and *Sumerland* may also be purchased at:

http://www.Amazon.com